DEATH IS A DREAM

Suspended animation, the doctor had said, was a simple matter — now that the bugs were ironed out. 'You'll be safe here until we wake you, with the know-how to cure what's wrong.' Brad Stevens chose the long cold sleep: and, as the doctor predicted, it worked. There was, however, the matter of paying the fee at the future end of the line. For Brad, death had been a dream, but the awakening was an incredible nightmare . . .

E. C. TUBB

DEATH IS A DREAM

Complete and Unabridged

LINFORD
Leicester

First published in Great Britain

First Linford Edition
published 2007

British Library CIP Data

Tubb, E. C.
    Death is a dream.—Large print ed.—
Linford mystery library
    1. Cryonics—Fiction
    2. Detective and mystery stories
    3. Large type books
    I. Title
    823.9'14 [F]

    ISBN 978–1–84617–716–3

Published by
F. A. Thorpe (Publishing)
Anstey, Leicestershire

Set by Words & Graphics Ltd.
Anstey, Leicestershire
Printed and bound in Great Britain by
T. J. International Ltd., Padstow, Cornwall

This book is printed on acid-free paper

To Linda

1

Tog Halsen, scavenger extraordinary, glowered as he stared into his immediate future. Everyone knew that he was one of the best in the business but, unless he had a break and soon, that reputation wouldn't last. He had failed twice running. If he failed again it would be hard to find backers, good workers, decent equipment and official assistance. He had seen it happen to others. He would drop to scraping a living on a contingent basis, trying to cut corners and dodge safety factors.

And that, he thought grimly, was the beginning of the end.

Tiredly the scavenger stretched and looked at the maps on his field desk. Damn all retros anyway. He had the growing conviction that he had been conned into something and he didn't like it. Not when his own neck was on the metaphorical block of financial execution.

Irritably he jerked to his feet and crossed the uneven ground of the camp. The thin column of smoke from the met-fire rose to one side but he ignored it. He timed his expeditions well and there was no immediate danger from southern winds — not unless nature had decided to change the habits of centuries. But the fire, the attendant and the fee for radioed weather reports were all added expenses. His scowl deepened as he approached the diggings.

'Where's Saul?'

'On the job.' A square man with a scarred face jerked his thumb towards a crumpled opening in a mound of vegetation-shrouded debris. Fresh-turned earth lay to either side and the white-clad figure of the Life Institute operator was busy with his culture plates.

'How long?' Tog didn't look at the lifeman. Sometimes official approval of a thing cost more than it was worth but you never knew when you might need a doctor.

'He's been gone about thirty minutes.' The scarred man glanced at the opening.

'He was just going to take a quick preliminary.' He grunted as a figure filled the opening. 'Here he comes now.'

Saul was a big man, bigger by reason of the padded body armour and protective helmet he wore. He pulled the respirator from his mouth, the glove from his right hand and wiped the back of it across his mouth. He looked dusty, tired and irritated. He shook his head at Tog's expression.

'No luck. It looks like it was a warehouse or a factory of some kind. The basement is holding up but I wouldn't like to gamble for how long. The upper structure has collapsed and only a few beams are supporting the weight.'

'Anything — '

'No.' Saul didn't wait for Tog to ask the inevitable question. 'Some junk machinery, boilers for heating. I think. Some packing cases, a little wire, a few heaps of rust. Some bones too,' he added as an afterthought. 'Not many — the rats could have been busy or not many made it in time. Not that it did them any good.' He shrugged at the scavenger's expression. 'Sorry, Tog, but there isn't a thing in there worth the trouble of digging out.'

'Damn!' Tog sensed the disappointment of his men and it added to his own. 'Is the structure what we're looking for?'

'No.' Saul was emphatic. 'The walls are concrete, the beams metal. The thing can't be more than four hundred years old.'

'No hewn stone? No overbuilding or incorporating of an older structure?'

'No.' Saul eased the helmet from his head. His hair was damp with perspiration. He didn't look at the scavenger. 'And nothing below, either. The floor is solid — I tested it with sonar. It's another bust, Tog.'

Another bust, two flopped expeditions and now this — still nothing after the sixth attempt despite the most careful planning and preliminary investigation. Tog looked down at his hands — they were clenched into fists at his sides. Deliberately he opened them, spreading and flexing the fingers, taking deep breaths to quell his anger.

'All right,' he decided. 'We'll have a

conference. Get cleaned up and report to my tent. You,' he snapped to the lifeman. 'Find that retro and report to me in an hour.' He was being impolite but things were too serious for him to worry about trifles. 'The rest of you scatter and see what you can find. Move!'

★   ★   ★

The retro was — arrogant. He came into the tent, tall, thin, emaciated with long hours of fasting and prayer, deep-set eyes in his tonsured skull burning with a fanatical light. Despite the chill of early spring open sandals framed dirty feet. He was naked beneath his habit. A massive crucifix hung from a leather belt. A rosary of large wooden beads hung from his hands.

Tog gestured towards a chair.

'Sit down, Elkan,' he said. 'You've — '

'My name is not Elkan.' His voice was harsh and acrid. 'I am Brother Ambrose of the Most Holy Order of — '

'All right,' snapped Tog. 'I know who you are.'

He felt his anger rising and fought for control. Damn these retros! It was one thing to have memories, he had them himself, but to live literally in a previous existence was something he couldn't understand. And, from the look of Elkan, it hadn't been such a wonderful time. Nothing but fasting and prayer. He shook his head. Such thoughts were getting him nowhere.

'You have failed,' said Brother Ambrose. His voice, his eyes, were scornful. 'Six times you have tried and each time the hand of Satan has misguided your efforts. Once again I exhort you to — '

'Satan had nothing to do with it,' snapped Tog bitterly. 'Not unless you are he. I followed your guidance and drew a bust. Now it's time for us to talk.'

'Deeds, not words are needed here!' The retro lifted his rosary as if to break into another of his interminable diatribes. Tog slammed his hand on his desk.

'Shut up! If you start preaching at me again I'll shove that thing down your gullet! Now sit down and listen!'

His hands were clenched again and he

felt the tension of anger. It didn't help to know that the rage stemmed from fear. Fear of failure and what failure would mean. But rage was useless here — anger had never yet been an aid to the finding of loot.

'Now, Brother Ambrose,' he said quietly when the retrophile was seated. 'You lived in the first part of the sixteenth century and were a monk at the monastery attached to the abbey of Waltham. Is that correct?'

'It is.'

'Please continue.'

Brother Ambrose looked surprised. He glanced at the lifeman seated at his side, looked at the dour face of Saul and let his eyes rest on Tog's grim features. For a moment the scavenger thought he was going to protest then he swallowed and shrugged.

'Life at the monastery was very — satisfying. It — but never mind that, you would not be interested. Sufficient to say that Waltham Abbey was not without those who sought to aid Mother Church. Many generous benefactors deeded gifts of land and money. There were other gifts of gold and precious stones — but enough of that. The hand of Satan made itself manifest in the antichrist Henry the Eighth. In 1539 came the general dissolution of the monasteries. Father Abbot took obvious precautions.'

'You are certain as to that?'

'Of course. I was there. I and two other brothers were entrusted with the task of safeguarding much of the altar furniture together with other precious objects. We buried them deep beneath the walls of the chapter house, sealing them with stone and mortar, piling earth so as to hide what we had done. Then we waited with prayer and fasting for the coming of the hordes of Satan who — '

'Never mind that,' said Tog hastily. 'We know what happened then.' He glanced at the lifeman. 'Truth?'

'Without question. You have our sworn attestation as to that.'

The scavenger nodded. Without it he wouldn't have given this project a second thought. The retro was genuine enough, the Life Institute had made sure of that, but one man's memory was a risky thing on which to chance the future.

Especially when that memory was stretched over eight hundred years.

With death and rebirth in between.

'The loot,' he said. 'The treasure. Tell me about it again.'

'There is a monstrance,' said the retro dreamily. 'Of pure gold heavier than a man can easily lift, studded with three hundred and sixty-five precious gems. A crucifix of silver edged with gold and inlaid with costly stones. Two incense boats and many plates of gold and silver. There is a wealth of chains and brooches — offerings from the faithful. There — it took many hours for the three of us to carry the treasure to where we buried it.'

'And?'

'There is a reliquary containing a fragment of bone from the blessed St Stephen. That is my reward for leading you to the treasure.'

'You can have it,' said Tog moodily. 'If we find it.' He leaned back and scowled at the maps littering his desk. Too few, too undetailed, too frustrating. Waltham

Abbey was the name of a place to the north of London — but just where was the abbey?

It was easy enough to point to a place on a map and give the answer but that was no help at all. Not when the maps were three hundred and fifty years out of date. Not when the very terrain had altered since then and landmarks had vanished. The maps were almost useless and the memory of the retro even more so.

The forests of early England had yielded to open fields and encroaching hamlets, the hamlets to villages and the whole engulfed in the brick tide of London. Then the woods had returned so that, now, verdure stood where streets had wound and even the hills had altered. No, he could not blame the retro — but he had relied on him.

He rose and strode to the open flap of the tent and stood staring outside. He had made a mistake, a bad one and he would have to pay for it. Here, on the outskirts, not even the general run of loot could be expected. Here had stood suburbs and small factories, dormitories for the workers of London. They could probe for years and find not even the cost.

Someone moved behind him. The retro stood at his side.

'You will try again,' said Brother Ambrose. 'The lifeman has agreed to help me remember. The reliquary must be found.'

Tog nodded, not answering, listening to the distant sounds his men made as they searched. He had always despised the shotgun technique. Good loot couldn't be found that way, the laws of chance and reason were against it. He liked the sharpshooter technique much better. The tracking down of probable loot, the organizing of an expedition, the probes and tests and then, with luck, the strike.

But there had been no strike for too long and now, he knew, his reputation was over. A scavenger lived by his luck.

'The reliquary.' Brother Ambrose was insistent. Tog cut him short.

'We will try one more time,' he said. 'If you agree to go into deep-hypnosis, track in trance — and if you can guarantee the basic cost.' He turned to where the lifeman sat with the patience of his profession. 'He can arrange the details.'

'But — '

'Shut up!' Tog brushed aside the other's protest. He leaned forward, head tilted a little, listening.

'You can't do this to me!' The retro was desperate. 'You — '

'Hold your tongue!' This time the sounds were louder, more distinct. Tog stepped forward as a man burst into the camp. He was sweating, his face red with effort, but he was grinning too.

'Tog!' he shouted. 'Saul! Come quick! We've found something!'

★   ★   ★

It was a hole but a hole rimmed with metal and sealed by a door. It rested in a pit which had been dug with furious haste and a man crouched over it, burner in hand, the flame spreading as it bit into the metal. Another stood, sonar in hand, listening to echoes.

'Give me that.' Saul snatched the instrument, clamped earphones over his head, frowned as he made adjustments. 'Quiet!' he yelled. 'All of you, shut up!'

In the silence the thin trickle of falling soil sounded very loud.

'It's hollow.' Saul handed back the instrument. 'Who found it?'

'I did.' A man thrust his way forward. 'I was probing around with a rod.' He lifted a thin shaft of weighted steel. 'The place looked promising so I gave it the works.' He gave a little chuckle, semi-intoxicated with his find. 'I don't know what made me stick at it so long. Instinct, I guess.'

Tog nodded, eyes narrowed as he surveyed the area. A good scavenger needed a nose for loot and he employed only the best.

'Keep working at that door,' he ordered. 'Let me know when it's open.' He stepped back, Saul close at his heels, ignoring the excited babble rising from the men. 'What do you think of it, Saul?'

'It could be a find.' The probeman searched the area with experienced eyes. 'The upper structure's fallen but that's natural — the trees would see to that, but that door looks as if it was built to last. Rust-proof alloy and well mounted in thick concrete and, from what I could tell from the sonar, the interior is clean.'

'Strong roof?'

'It would have to be to stand that weight.' Saul looked at the hill of debris, the thick roots of encroaching trees, the weight of almost four centuries. 'A tall building,' he mused. 'Four, maybe six storeys, and if it was recent that means lots of reinforced concrete and plenty of mass.' He shrugged. 'It could be another bomb-proof,' he pointed out. 'Full of bones and nothing else.'

'So far from the centre?'

'It could be.' Saul shrugged again. 'Well, we'll soon know.'

It took twenty minutes to burn open the door and, fast as Saul was, the guildsman was faster. He waved them back as, hooded and shapeless in protective clothing, he advanced with his geigers. Carefully he tested the area, thrust himself through the opening, vanished from view. The men of the

Power Guild had never lacked courage.

'It's clean,' he said five minutes later. He'd thrown back his hood and breathed gratefully of the cool air. 'Residual stuff only and it falls off from the opening. It's all yours, Tog, but remember to call me if you break into anything new.'

Tog grunted, already fastening the protective armour which the engineers claimed would withstand half a ton of falling debris. Quickly he followed Saul into the opening then halted as the probesman inched ahead. This was no time for impatience.

'Firm,' said Saul, his voice echoing. 'Built to last.'

'What's ahead?'

'Looks like a maze. It could be a bomb-proof, Tog. Most of them were built with similar radiation-baffles.' His light shone from the roof. 'As solid as the day it was built. Reinforced concrete by the look of it, you can see the marks of the shuttering. I wonder — ?' Metallic noises and the sudden stutter of a burner filled the air. Hastily Tog adjusted his respirator.

15

'What are you doing?'

'Testing the wall. I read somewhere that — ' Saul gave a satisfied grunt. 'Tog! This wall's filled with lead!'

'Lead?' Lead was money. Saul stepped back as the scavenger thrust forward, his light shining into the charred, greyish hole. He dug at the metal which was sandwiched between walls of concrete. 'You're right! There must be tons of it!' Tog felt a tremendous relief. If all the walls were similar — He stopped dreaming. 'What's ahead?'

There were narrow corridors and sealed doors. They burned them open and waited impatiently as the guildsman checked for radiation. There was no radiation but, in the heart of the underground structure, they found something else.

Something incredible.

2

Edward Maine, Master of Hypnotic Therapy, Comptroller of the Life Institute, South-East Region leaned on the low parapet of the upper promenade of the Lifetower and stared thoughtfully towards the setting sun. Behind him a novice stood in respectful attendance. Maine ignored him. He had other things on his mind.

It hadn't rained for ten days now and, during all that time, the wind had blown steadily from the west yet still the radiation monitors remained silent. It could only mean one thing. Soon now the great necropolis of London would be ready for safe entry, the mouldering ruins no longer the prerogative of daring scavengers but open to all for systematic looting.

The prospect was intoxicating. No one could guess the wealth of knowledge resting in the wilderness of brick and stone but there was no doubt that the value of salvagable material would be fabulous. During his few moments of relaxation Maine liked to imagine what it would be. Metal, rare stones, forgotten mechanical techniques — the list was endless. Thinking about it he leaned a little farther over the parapet and sensed rather than felt the novice at his side.

'I'm not going to fall, young man.'

'No, sir.' The novice was young, very conscious of his duties, very proud at having been attached to the retinue of the Comptroller. But he stayed close to his master's side.

Maine sighed, half-tempted to keep the young man in suspense, then sighed again as he recognized the petty application of authority. He stepped back from the edge and immediately noted the signals of relief.

'Your emotions are showing,' he said coldly. 'You must practise better self-control. You must always remember that, no matter what you feel, your patients must never know it. You recognize your fault?'

'Yes, sir. I feared for your safety and — '

'You feared!' snapped Maine. 'And you displayed relief at the removal of that fear. Such emotions must never be revealed. Assurance, yes; confidence, certainly; fear, doubt, anxiety, never. Such emotions are destructive. Do you understand?'

'Yes, sir.'

'Good. See that you remember it.'

'I will, sir, and — thank you.'

The novice was sincere. Maine was a hard master but one of the best. A lesser man would have broken him for his fault — but then a lesser man might never have spotted the fault at all. And the Comptroller was right. If a lifeman could not control himself how could he hope to control others?

'To work,' said Maine, dismissing the incident. 'I want you to send for two companions from the psychiatric wards. They are to be strong, agile and skilled at visual diagnosis. They are to attend me here but to remain unobtrusive. Select them with care. I will not tolerate any failure.'

'You are completing the treatment, sir?'

'Yes. There is no point in further delay.'

The novice nodded, walked to a communicator, spoke into it. He looked at Maine. 'Do you expect trouble, sir?'

'No, but it would be foolish to risk the work of months by neglecting an elementary precaution.'

'I understand, sir.' The novice turned back to the communicator, listened, spoke, broke the connection. 'Fifteen minutes, sir. Is that satisfactory?'

'It will do,' said Maine casually. 'There is no great hurry.' The corners of his mouth lifted in a shallow smile. 'After all, he has waited so long that a few more minutes won't hurt him.'

★   ★   ★

He had waited three hundred and thirty-eight years.

His name was Brad Stevens. He was an atomic physicist, tall, thin, scholastically handsome. He was forty-two years of age — correction, he had been born in the year 1937.

How old was he now?

He sat in a little room on a soft chair

20

and stared between his knees at a floor covered with seamless plastic. The plastic held a a pattern of abstract swirls and unconnected curves so that it was easy to let his mind drift and allow the pattern to take on familiar shapes and recognizable forms. Things and buildings, flowers and — faces.

Sir Wiliam's face.

' . . . *sorry to have to tell you this but you're man enough to take the truth. There is no possibility of successful surgery. I can ease things a little with drugs but . . .* '

The Queen's surgeon. Old, kind, sympathetic but devoid of hope. He vanished in the swirls and another took his place. A strong face. Square-jawed, hard, dynamic, the planes carved from stone. The face of a man who had learned to face harsh reality.

Edgar Cranstead, Director of Atomic Research. The real Director — not the political puppet who stalked in borrowed glory.

' . . . *give you a choice. You can live out your life knowing what's to come and* what the end will be or you can take a chance. You can go into the Cradle. The choice is yours.'

Choice!

There had been no real choice. To live out the rest of his life under constant surveillance or to take the chance offered that, one day, a cure might be found for the cancer eating into his body. The government was willing to give him that chance for the sake of the knowledge he carried in his brain, the skills he possessed. A short life and a painful death or —

He had chosen the Cradle.

'*An appropriate name, don't you think?*' Doctor Lynne smiled up at him from the patterned floor. '*Some of the boys wanted to name it the Tomb but that was a little too macabre. Don't you agree?*'

He had agreed.

'*Suspended animation,*' continued the doctor. '*Simple, really, once we managed to iron out the bugs. Just a matter of slowing down the metabolism to almost zero and keeping it that way.*' He beat his hand against a wall. '*This place is built like a vault. You'll be safe enough in here until we wake you and, when we do, we'll have the know-how to cure what's wrong. All you have to do is to go to sleep and, when you wake, your troubles will be over.*'

Well, he was awake.

He looked up from the memory-triggering patterns on the floor, conscious of a sudden, tremendous glow of life.

He was awake!

And he had a second chance!

★   ★   ★

A novice escorted him upstairs, falling behind as they reached the promenade, standing silent and watchful as Brad looked at the city.

'You are disappointed?' Maine, thought Brad, seemed to have the uncanny knack of reading minds. Or perhaps it was just that he had trained himself to read the most minute change of expression.

'A little,' he admitted. He looked again over the city, a part of his mind wondering at the absence of noise, another part supplying the answer. Electric power, clean and silent. The buildings were unambitious. Flat-roofed, some tiered, the majority low with here and there a tower reaching towards the sky.

Phoenix was neat enough — but it didn't seem much for three hundred years of progress. He said so. Maine shrugged.

'Perhaps. But the progress of your time was somewhat violently interrupted. You know that.'

'Yes,' Brad agreed. 'I know it.'

It was, he thought, surprising just how much he did know about this new age. Little, everyday things had caused no embarrassment. He knew the rank and purpose of those whom he met. He knew how to operate various devices with their unfamiliar controls. Even the distortions of the language presented no problem.

Obviously he had been taught and they must have done it before he awoke.

It had been a strange awakening. He remembered a time of confusion like a distorted dream when he had lain wrapped in an endless darkness which had rocked and lulled him to tranquillity. The amniotic tank, of course, he knew that now — simulacrum of a womb. It had shielded him and protected him while he regained his strength and there had been a voice, deep and compelling, commanding and directing him through the trauma of birth.

The trauma of birth!

Now why should he think of a thing like that?

The air was warm with the sultry heat of late summer but here, high on the tower, there was a refreshing breeze from the west. Brad stepped closer to the edge of the parapet, resting his elbows on the stone, leaning over as he stared below.

From the wall behind him two men stepped forward, their eyes watchful. Impatiently Maine waved them back and joined Brad where he stood. The novice ignored the command. He was a shadow behind them both. Coincidence gave Brad's comment an added depth.

'I'm not going to fall over, young man.'

'No,' said Maine. 'I don't think that you will — now.'

'Did you think that I might?'

'The death-wish can be very strong,' said the Comptroller. 'You are fresh from the comfort of the womb, faced with the necessity of adjusting to a new age — in many ways, perhaps, a frightening age. Many would choose not to face it.'

'I'm not one of them.' Brad drew a deep breath into his lungs, enjoying the taste and smell of it, the feeling of life it gave. 'I like life too well to want to end it before I have to. You don't have to worry about me.'

Maine remained silent, his eyes searching the other's face. Brad didn't turn.

'Tell me about it,' he said quietly. The Comptroller knew what he meant.

'The Débâcle came about fifteen years after you entered the vault,' he said. 'In the following period of chaos much was forgotten, including your resting place. Not that it mattered — the radioactivity precluded entry into the area. But your engineers built well and the structure was basically unharmed.'

'And?'

'The vault was found by some scavengers guided by a retro who claimed to have knowledge of the whereabouts of buried treasure. They did not find the treasure. Instead they found your vault. It contained, among other things, thirty-seven capsules, eleven of which were found to still contain viable life. We managed to resurrect three.'

'Three?'

'Yes,' said Maine calmly. 'You have two companions from your own age.'

★   ★   ★

The young man was Carl Holden. He was big with a rugger-player's physique, about twenty-eight years old, with golden, close-cropped hair. He waved to Brad as he lounged in a chair.

'Hi, pal!'

Brad ignored him, his eyes unbelieving as he stared at the woman.

'Helen!'

'Brad! Oh, Brad!' Their hands met, squeezed, lingered before falling apart.

'Brad! How wonderful!'

'Didn't you know?'

'They said there was another but not who.' She gave a little laugh of delight. 'Brad! I can't believe it!'

It was coincidence but not as outrageous as it seemed. They had worked at the same place, Helen in the biochemical laboratories, and had had the same boss. She too must have — ?

'Leukaemia,' she said. 'About two years after you went abroad.' She smiled at his expression. 'That's what the answer was when I asked after you. A special assignment, very hush-hush, questions not wanted and answers not given. The Security of the Nation depended on utter secrecy and all that rot. Anyway, when I fell sick — but I'm forgetting! You know the drill.'

'Yes,' he said. 'Are you all right now?'

'Of course. They filled me with dope and told me that twenty years would see me better than new and twice as beautiful. Were they right, Brad?'

'Yes,' he said. Helen Shapparch was a beautiful woman. She had always been

28

beautiful. Once — but that was more than three hundred years ago. No torch could burn that long.

'When you two love-birds have finished,' said Carl. He sounded peevish and Brad guessed that he felt a little jealous. 'Maybe we can get down to business. When did they stick you in the Cradle?'

' '69. You?'

'Two years earlier. I was the first after they revived the five-year dog and found it could be done. I had the same trouble as Helen, only they told me ten years not twenty. The damn liars!'

'You're living,' said Brad curtly. 'Be thankful for that. The others didn't have our luck.'

'So I'm living!' Carl jerked from his chair and paced the floor. 'So when do I start? I want to get out of here and start catching up. If these quacks think that I'm going to be one of their prize exhibits then they want to think again. I've had enough of hospitals to last me this and every other life.'

'That's an odd way to put it,' said Brad.

'That's the only way to put it. A new

age. A new way of looking at things. Or don't you believe in reincarnation?'

'What he believes doesn't matter,' interrupted Helen. 'You forget that we've had longer to think about things than he has. But we're wasting time. I think that Maine put us together so that we could make some kind of plans for the future. What do you think, Brad?'

'Why ask him?'

'Be quiet, Carl. Well, Brad?'

Her faith in his ability to provide the answers flattered his ego but did little more than that. But the problem had to be faced. They were alive and had to go on living. How was something else.

'We can only go by analogy,' he said slowly. 'If, in our time, a group of people had somehow survived from the seventeenth century, what would we have done for them? I think that they would have been given some kind of government support or, at least, a private trust would have been set up to provide for them. In return they would have provided information about their era. They — '

He broke off as a chime quivered the

air. A flat envelope dropped through a slot beside the door.

'Mail delivery.' Carl crossed the room, stooped to pick it up. Helen frowned as he passed her.

'Never mind that now, Carl. Go on, Brad.'

'Well — ' He frowned with thought. Why did she have to look at him with such trusting eyes? 'They would have given lectures, things like that. In any case we can be certain that we wouldn't have let them want for anything. I think it fair to assume that this society will feel much the same. After all, they have a responsibility towards us and — '

'Rubbish!'

'What — ?'

'Rubbish,' snapped Carl again. 'What you are saying is sheer balderdash and you must know it. What we would have done,' he mimicked. 'Jesus Christ! Do you think that every society must be as soft as ours?'

He stood before them, his face red, his blue eyes gleaming with anger.

He held some papers in his big hand.

'How stupid can you get?' Carl gestured with the papers. 'Here you are saying how humane these people must be and all the time you don't know a damn thing about them. Well, take this and be educated!'

He thrust one of the papers at Helen, the other at Brad. Slowly he took it. The typescript was a little unfamiliar but the arrangement was unmistakable.

It was a bill and the total was incredible.

3

The street was over two hundred years old which meant that all the houses had the same monotonous bubble-shape, hemispheres of rough-cast concrete unrelieved by any attempt at decoration. Only the most fanatical retrophile would want to keep it intact, for it could hold few pleasant memories. For Captain Westdale it held none at all. He was no romanticist and did not care for slums.

Shuman lived in one of the houses. He jerked open the door as Serge pressed the button, his sharp, fox-face creased in a smile of welcome.

'Ah, Captain. I have been waiting for you. We are a little late, are we not?'

He spoke with a soothing tone of condescension which, despite the organ-tones of his voice, irritated his visitor to the point of fury because he knew the reason for it. Serge Westdale was a policeman. He did not wear a uniform and he didn't direct traffic or guard public places but he carried a badge and was sworn to uphold the law. The hypnotist wasn't impressed. To him Serge was a cripple.

He led the way into the interior of the house as Serge muttered apologies, wishing that he didn't have to deal with the man and hoping that, at least, his reputation was not exaggerated. As yet he had no proof of that but he had to be fair. It was asking a lot of this back-street practitioner, unlicensed by the Institute, to succeed where top-qualified men had failed.

Automatically Serge relaxed on the couch, watching Shuman set up his hypnotics, hoping, despite his foreboding, that this time something positive would happen. The hypnotist, he noted, was sweating. He was also surprisingly clumsy. It was a combination which aroused his suspicions.

'What are you planning to do this session?'

'Place you under deep hypnosis and crash the Barrier.'

'You tried to do that the last time.' Serge swung long legs over the edge of the couch. 'You had no success then — what makes you think that you'll have it now?'

'Please leave the technical details to me!' snapped Shuman. He dabbed at his forehead with a dingy handkerchief and gave a rueful smile. 'Please forgive my sharpness but, professional pride — you know how it is.'

'No, I don't know.' Serge was curt. There was too much at stake for him to be careless. 'The last time you said that perhaps I was a new-birth and that to try and crash the Barrier was a waste of time.'

'That is true and a possibility we must not disregard. However, as I said, I wish to make certain. New-births are extremely rare. Now please relax and leave everything to me. Success is impossible without the fullest co-operation.'

'A moment, lifeman.' Serge made the title sound like an insult. 'I want us both to be quite clear on this. You know the penalties for implanting false memories?'

'Naturally.'

'Then I take it that your recorder is sealed and operating?'

'Of course.'

'And that your check-cameras are the same?'

'Really, Captain, I would hardly — '

'I think that you would do almost anything to earn the thousand contingent fee.' Serge was brutal. 'Give me waking audit as usual.'

'It would be a waste of time.' Shuman recovered his composure and with it some of his dignity. 'We have tried that and it simply does not work. Your memories are too deeply implanted, the Barrier is too strong for such techniques. You may even, as I mentioned, be a new-birth. It will take the deepest hypnosis and shocktactics to find out.'

It was tempting to agree, to place himself without reservation into the other's hands, but he dared not take the risk. Not with this quack eager for money and who might risk his neck to earn it. Decisively Serge shook his head.

'Nothing doing. Waking audit as usual.'

'But, Captain — '

'One hundred for your trouble,' Serge interrupted and wondered at his charity. 'If you manage Breakthrough I'll give you the thousand as promised. Take it or leave it.'

Shuman sighed, some of the anxiety fading from his eyes at the certainty of some money at least. He looked at the dingy wall, the antiquated equipment, the meter clocking up his power-charges.

'Could you make that a hundred and fifty, Captain? Unless I pay the Power Guild soon I'll — '

'All right. Now get on with it.'

It was a long session. Shuman, licensed or not, knew his business and he was grateful enough to do his best. He used every trick in the book and a few of his own devising. He took Serge back through youth, through childhood, through infancy and then, in the foetal stage, he stuck.

The trauma was too great. He couldn't achieve Breakthrough. The Barrier remained inviolate.

Serge was still a cripple.

★　★　★

Police Headquarters were on Prime Avenue and Serge drove to his office at the regulated twenty-five miles an hour, not remembering, when he swung into the parking lot, a thing about his journey.

Grenmae lounged in his chair reading his usual book and Serge wondered just what attraction Boswell's autobiography held for the man. True, he had lived in the period but there must be a limit to nostalgia. He said so and Grenmae shook his head.

'It isn't that, Serge. It's fun to read about the era and it helps me to remember but I'm no candidate for Facsimile. You can't live in those places unless you've plenty of money and I haven't. I'd wind up as an ostler or a lackey like I was before and I had enough of that kind of life then without wanting more of the same now.' He closed the book and slid it into a drawer. 'Any luck, Serge?'

'No.'

'That's tough.' Grenmae was genuinely sympathetic. 'But what else did you expect from a quack? A miracle?'

Serge shrugged. There was no embar-rassment in discussing his disability. In an age where men had experienced a thousand different periods of existence, toleration had acquired a real meaning.

'What you need is a top-operator from the Life Institute,' said Grenmae. 'Maine or Clowder. They're among the best.'

'At their prices they should be. I can't afford what they ask.'

'You could always arrange a mortgage.' Grenmae suggested. Then, as he saw the captain's expression, 'No, well I guess you know best. It's your business.'

'That's right.' Serge changed the subject. 'Anything interesting?'

'Nothing much. A pickpocket was caught over in the market and we had to rescue him from the mob. A couple of youngsters jumped their governors and raced down Tenth Avenue. A man was beaten and robbed in Homer Road but he'll live. A — '

'Homer Road? Isn't that near Alsatia?'

'Right on the edge.'

'Then he asked for it. It's none of our business anyway if he didn't get himself killed. Anything else?'

'A looper did a dutch and there was a chasing over in the third sector, but that's about all.'

'A chasing!' Serge frowned. He hated the sudden, unpredictable violence that, for some unknown reason, sent a panic-stricken quarry fleeing from a growing, hysterical mob. 'Did they get him?'

'Her,' corrected Grenmae. 'It was a woman. No, they didn't get her, we managed to rescue her in time.'

'Good.' Serge relaxed as he stared at the pin-marked map. A normal day, nothing to worry about and nothing which immediately concerned him. The financial department would take care of the pickpocket and the victim of the chase. The beaten man had no redress. The two racers would be penalized under the general safety regulations. Nothing could be done about the looper.

A quiet, uneventful day.

He caught Grenmae's smile.

'Is that all?'

'One other small, trifling matter.' Grenmae seemed to be enjoying a private joke. He took a slip from his desk and passed it to the captain. 'The major wants you to go to the Institute and act as adjudicator.'

'He does?' Serge frowned as he read the slip in his hand. 'What's this got to do with me? Adjudication of debt has nothing to do with my department.'

'Maybe not,' agreed Grenmae. 'But the Old Man thought you should handle this one. It concerns those three suspended animation cases and he reckons that makes it your business.'

Serge grunted. Sometimes the major carried logic too far.

★   ★   ★

They were waiting when he arrived. The three of them in chairs against one wall, the recorder and the Chief Accountant. Serge nodded to them then looked at the sleepers. They seemed normal enough, taller and a little heavier than most and the woman — the woman was beautiful.

Brad heard Helen's sharp whisper.

'He looks too young to be a good lawyer.'

'He isn't a lawyer. Maine explained it to me. He's a policeman, some kind of special officer. Handsome, isn't he?'

Helen didn't answer but Brad had seen the look the officer had given her. Inwardly he smiled. They had at least one ally — at least, Helen did.

'Let's hope that he's fighting on our side,' muttered Carl. 'Just look at Crow's face. Talk about Shylock!'

Chief Accountant Crow was no lover of Shakespeare and knew nothing of the infamous moneylender but he was equally adamant as to his due. The Institute was owed money and he intended to collect it. Serge agreed with the debt but disputed the amount.

'This prior item,' he said. 'You paid the scavengers 500 imperials each for thirty-six unopened capsules — a total of 18,000, yet you have split this sum between my clients — 6,000 each. This is unjust. They should be charged no more than the cost of their individual capsules.'

'I disagree. The money was paid and, because of it, these three are now alive.'

'Yet you purchased the capsules on an

individual basis,' insisted Serge. 'You did not buy them in bulk nor did you finance the expedition. My point remains valid.'

He relaxed as Crow reluctantly nodded agreement. It was the first victory but he doubted if he would win many others. Crow was too shrewd for that. But he had to try.

'I must question this item,' continued Serge. 'You have charged the entire cost of the total resurrection — operation — to my clients. This seems unjust in view of the fact that eight failures resulted from eleven attempts.'

'Are you suggesting that we *pro rata* the charges?'

'Yes.'

'I cannot agree. It was because of the knowledge gained from those failures that we finally managed to succeed.'

'My clients cannot be expected to pay for your tuition,' snapped the captain. Crow lifted his hand.

'One moment, please. Let us be rational about this. If you came to me with a disease which was unfamiliar to me and I managed to cure it — would you feel it unfair that you were asked to pay the cost of basic research?'

Serge hesitated, recognizing the trap, and for a moment was tempted to yield the point. Then he looked at Helen and continued the battle.

'If the facts were made clear to me from the beginning then, of course, I could have no complaint. But my clients were not so informed. They did not have free choice and it is unjust to charge them for expenses over which they had no control. Therefore I — '

Carl leaned across Helen, his head almost touching her cheek and he whispered to Brad.

'This is crazy! Those guys will be asking us to pay for the building next on the grounds that we couldn't have been treated until it was erected.'

'That was covered in the charges for the accommodation,' said Brad. 'They run this place like a hotel. It's fair enough when you think about it.'

'Fair, my eye!'

Carl was annoyed but paying for medical attention was nothing new. What was both new and disturbing was the manner of disputing the bill and the seriousness of the discussion. It was almost as if they were on trial and Serge was a lawyer trying to reduce the penalty for their crime.

Money, thought Brad grimly, still retained its tremendous importance.

'He's winning,' breathed Helen. 'Look at the fat man, he's giving in.'

Crow had finally yielded the point, looking sourly at the recorder as the woman amended the bills, then glanced at the policeman with reluctant admiration.

'You are a hard man, Captain, but I still think you argued from faulty premises.'

'We can take it to the courts if you wish,' suggested Serge. Crow dismissed the notion with a wave of his hand.

'No, I'll accept your argument because it's a borderline case. Now, as to the other items — '

Serge gained no further victories nor had he expected to. Medication, care, food and attention were all listed at regular prices but he did raise his eyebrows at the specialist's fees. Crow was quick to pounce.

'Even you would hardly dare to claim

that these were simple cases,' he said. 'Master Hypnotist Maine worked at intensive pressure for long periods and used his skill to the uttermost. Also there would have been no hope of return had he been unsuccessful. Therefore the fees are on a contingent basis which — '

'No dispute,' interrupted Serge. He relaxed and smiled at the accountant. 'We'll accept the rest without protest.'

He studied the three against the wall as the recorder busied herself amending the documents, a little curious but not intensely so. They remembered a time long in the past but that was not unusual. They were a little vague as to present-day customs but he had known retrophiles equally so. There was nothing particularly special about them at all except that — well, it was hard not to stare at the woman.

She met his eyes and smiled at him as she extended her hand.

'You did a good job,' said Helen, and introduced herself. 'This is Brad Stevens and this is Carl Holden.'

'Serge Westdale, captain of temporal

police, South-east Region.'

'Temporal?' Helen looked surprised. 'That means time, doesn't it? Well, now I know why you're here. I suppose we're time travellers, in a way, so we'd come under your jurisdiction. But surely you don't just sit around waiting for people like us to be discovered?'

'Of course not.' He knew that she was waiting for him to explain but felt disinclined to go into detail. 'My work is — different.'

'A secret?'

'No, it's just that — ' He turned as Crow called to him to attend to the formalities. They didn't take long. He handed each of them a copy of the revised account. 'Hold on to these, they're important. It's a certified copy of your debt to the Life Institute together with interest rates and limitations of repayment period.'

'That's nice,' said Carl. He scowled down at the document. 'What are we supposed to pay with — blood?'

'He's got a point,' said Brad. He felt a little sick. Apparently they were to be discharged from the Institute with no money, no home, nowhere to go and no obvious future. As a start to a new life it was hardly promising.

It was also a little frightening that none of the others seemed to consider it at all unusual.

'You and your dreams,' sneered Carl to Brad. 'You said that they'd look after us. Like hell they will! They don't give a damn!'

'I don't understand?' Crow was genuinely bewildered. 'Surely you don't expect the Institute to accept the responsibility of your future welfare? You are certified fit, whole and able — the rest is up to yourselves.'

'And if we starve in the gutter how the hell do you expect to get paid?' Carl was flaming with anger. 'Sell our bodies for dogmeat?'

'Not for animal food,' protested Crow. 'That would be uneconomical. But — '

'All right,' interrupted Serge flatly. 'You can use my place until you get established.'

He was, he thought, a little crazy. These

people weren't children. They were not helpless. They were adults with an adult's skill and responsibility and they had brains and the will to exist. It should be enough.

He was a fool to be so charitable.

4

The Khan Employment Agency reminded Brad of a charity-doctor's surgery. There was the same dingy room, the same hard benches containing the same collection of men and women all suffering from the same disease. The disease was poverty and the doctor, instead of treating their physical ills, was interested only in finding them a job.

At a fee.

'One imperial,' snapped the hard-faced woman in reception. 'That's the interview fee. Ten per cent of all pay for any job we may find you. Pay now, please.'

Slowly Brad handed over some of the money he had borrowed from the captain.

'Do I get it back if the interview's a bust?'

It was a silly question. Tiredly he sat down and waited his turn. A bell sounded. He rose, entered an inner room which stank of must and mildew, stale smoke and edible grease. A withered man sat behind a knee-hole desk. He wore a high, starched collar, a flowing cravat, a frock-coat and steel-rimmed pince-nez. He waved Brad to a chair and solemnly took a pinch of snuff.

Mr. Khan, Brad guessed, had been a solicitor in a previous existence and couldn't forget it.

'Ah, Stevens,' he said, and looked down to where Brad's application rested on a blotter. His voice was thin, dry and precise. His eyes, as they peered at Brad over the ridiculous lenses, were small, blue and very shrewd. 'Atomic physicist?'

'That's right.'

'I see.' Thin fingers rapped delicately on the lid of the snuff box. 'Why have you come to me? Why not to the Guild?'

'I've been to the Guild. They weren't interested.' In fact they had treated Brad as a medieval Christian would have treated Judas. 'They seem to blame me for what happened.'

'The Débâcle?' Khan shrugged. 'Natural enough, perhaps, but surely they are interested in what you can tell them about the generation of power?'

He was, thought Brad, having himself a little fun. With difficulty he kept his temper.

'We don't speak the same language,' he said. 'I talk of tons and they talk of ounces. The power-needs of society aren't the same as they were in my day. And they seem to be afraid of atomics as I know it.'

'But surely you could teach them something?'

'I could,' said Brad bitterly. 'If only what not to do but — they don't seem to trust me.'

'No,' said Khan. 'And they know what not to do.' Slowly he took another pinch of snuff. 'Tell me,' he said casually, 'could you make a bomb?'

'An atomic bomb? Yes, if I had the material. Why?'

'Perhaps that's why they don't trust you.' Khan gave a bland smile. 'You lived in London, I understand.'

'Yes.'

'Interesting. Did you know Furnivals Inn?'

'No.' Brad tried to restrain his impatience. 'They demolished it before I was born.'

'A pity, I had an office there.' Khan sighed as if at a pleasant memory. 'Brave times, Stevens, brave times.'

'I know the site,' said Brad hastily. 'But I only remember modern London, the one just before the Débâcle.' He anticipated the next question. 'And I have no memory of any previous existence.'

'A cripple?' Khan tutted his sympathy. Brad shook his head.

'I don't know. No one has yet tried to — ' It seemed ridiculous to talk about. 'In my time we didn't believe in reincarnation.'

'That,' said Khan seriously, 'was the misfortune of the past.'

He leaned back, lips pursed as he stared at the dirty ceiling, fingertips tapping gently on the lid of his snuff box.

'You could make a bomb,' he mused softly. 'You could make killer-dusts and, of course, you know the half-lives of radio-active materials. You know much of what the Guild protects — and you are unattached.'

'Yes,' said Brad. He wondered what the little man was getting at. Khan didn't explain.

'Well,' he said cheerfully, swinging down his eyes, 'never mind all that for now. We have rather more immediate business to discuss. You have, of course, been to other agencies?'

Brad nodded.

'And they could not help you? I suspected as much. The trouble with big agencies is that they lack the human element. Computers, Stevens, have no heart and no sympathy and those who work with them seem to acquire the same attributes. But, to be fair, you fall in rather a difficult category.'

Brad readied himself for another rejection.

'I could probably find you a place in a labour squad,' said Khan. 'It doesn't pay much and — ' He saw Brad's expression. 'No? I can't blame you. Well, let us progress. Have you any other special talents? Can you sing, paint, play a musical instrument? Are you especially good at any sports or games or do anything — well — unusual?'

'No.'

'A pity.' The little man frowned, helped himself to snuff, dusted his stained cravat. 'You said that you knew London. Did you know it well?'

'I lived there most of my life.'

'I find that very interesting.' Khan suddenly took a great interest in his nails. 'Tell me, Stevens, where do you usually dine?'

'At home — when I dine at all.'

'I see.' Khan switched his attention to his other hand. 'They tell me the Folgone Terrace is an excellent place to eat. There is a wonderful view from the roof — and you meet the most interesting company.'

Brad grunted, wondering why the little man was being so cautious.

'The view is particularly good at about seven — or should I say nineteen hundred hours?'

'Seven will do. I'm old fashioned.'

Khan laughed with a dry rustling and Brad realized that he had made a joke.

'Old-fashioned!' Khan rustled. 'That's good! That's damned good! Stap me if it ain't!'

He had, thought Brad sourly, a peculiar sense of humour.

★ ★ ★

Seven found Brad standing outside the Folgone Terrace looking up at the glass-and-stone façade. He turned and bumped into a man. He was short, thick, dressed in the helmet and armour of a Roman Tribune of the time of Augustus Ceasar. He glared, one hand dropping to the hilt of his sword.

'Sorry,' said Brad.

The man said something — if it was Latin Brad didn't recognize more than a few sounds. Not surprising, really, in his own time no one had known how the Romans pronounced their dead language.

'Sorry,' he said again, then, '*Pace* — I mean *pax*.'

'Peace,' said the man thickly. He frowned as if in the throes of translation. 'You speak badly, barbarian. Have greater care when next you meet an officer of the Legions.'

'I will,' said Brad quickly. '*Vale!*'

'*Vale!*'

The man swung away, probably heading towards Londinium, the Roman Facsimile built higher up the river where they had reintroduced the old, gladiatorial games. Brad starcd after him, wondering what it was like to be a retrophile, to have such vivid memories of the past that they conquered those of the present, then he shrugged. He doubted if he would ever know. He wasn't sure that he ever wanted to.

A lift swept him up to a glass-walled restaurant whose entrancing odours brought saliva to his mouth and nostalgic twinges to his stomach. Hastily he climbed the stairs to the viewing platform above.

It was a flat, open square with a breast-high parapet, some benches, some coin-operated telescopes and nothing else. A scatter of people filled the area. A solitary guard leaned against the wall at the head of the stairs, one thumb hooked in his gunbelt, his eyes vacant as he chewed something with a bovine monotony.

Brad crossed to the parapet and stared down at the city. It seemed a normal enough place now that he was getting used to it. Only the wide variety of clothing worn by the people signalled the great difference between this society and the one he had known. Otherwise they were basically the same — heaven if you had money, hell if you didn't.

He caught a flash of red, the swirl of a scarlet cloak on the street below. Another Roman retro on his way to Londinium. Brad stared thoughtfully after the man. At college he had made the fencing team and should be able to hold his own in one of the gladiatorial combats. An épée wasn't a gladius but he would have the advantage of modern techniques and trained reflexes. If the worst came he could always use his skill for gain.

If things could possibly get any worse.

'A nice view, isn't it?'

The man had come from nowhere. Brad saw a thick-set body, drab clothing, a mat of beard over which stared hard, grey eyes.

'I'm Morgan,' he said. Brad smiled.

'Captain Morgan? Of the Spanish Main?'

'Who's he?'

'Forget it,' said Brad. 'It was a joke.'

Morgan grunted and narrowed his eyes.

'You Stevens?'

'Yes.'

'I thought so.' Morgan gestured towards the city. 'Seeing as how you're new maybe you'd like me to point out a few things. That tower over there, that's Carlton's Galleries, the biggest dealer in antiques in the region. Over there is Delancy's Financial Trust — he's the biggest shark in the business and over there, to the left of the Lifetower, that's the regional Headquarters of the Guild. Do themselves proud, don't they?'

There was an odd note in Morgan's voice. Brad accepted the bait.

'They shouldn't find that hard,' he said casually. 'From what I hear they've got it made.'

'You can say that again!' Morgan spat over the parapet. 'A man hasn't the chance to scrape a decent living with those parasites living on his back. What with power costs, geiger-fees, having to operate under supervision and paying percentages to the checkers the profit's gone before it's made.'

'I can imagine,' said Brad. 'You, of course, are a scavenger?'

'One of the best.'

Brad nodded, then lifted his arm and pointed to where a slender spire rose at the edge of the city. 'What's that place?'

'Marc Veldon's. Stay away from him. He's a ghoul.' Morgan sounded impatient. 'We were talking about the Guild.'

'So?'

'So maybe you've as much reason to dislike them as I have.' Morgan glanced over his shoulder and lowered his voice. 'You can't have had things easy since you woke. In this world, brother, money is life. Follow?'

'Keep talking.'

'You know London. Well, I know it too, but the maps are poor and we've never really gone in deep as yet.' He spat again. 'Those damn guildsmen! I've had three of them working for five days at a time before now checking a sector only to be told that it was too hot for working.'

'They should know,' said Brad. 'They

were warning you against risking your life.'

'Maybe.' Morgan was sour. 'Or maybe they were saving the sector for themselves. How do I know they were telling the truth?'

'You could check,' said Brad. 'You — ' He broke off, remembering. 'Does it make all that difference?'

'Not to me and the boys — we'd be willing to take our chances, but we've got to be sure of a good profit before taking a big risk. We want silver, diamonds, stuff like that. Antiques too. Understand?'

'I think so.'

'Good.' Morgan smiled and became very casual. 'Now where could we find diamonds? Do you know?'

Brad didn't answer. He was beginning to understand Morgan's interest. Like all treasure hunters the scavengers wanted small, compact, high-priced items. And he could lead them to where they could be found.

'How much?'

Morgan blinked then grinned with a flash of white teeth.

'You'll play?'

'For a price. I can tell you where to find what you're looking for. I'll draw maps and diagrams and — ' He broke off as Morgan shook his head. 'What now?'

'I want more than maps. I want you to act as guide.'

'All right.' It was decent, respectable work and carried the possibility of high rewards. 'When do I start?'

'Well, now,' said Morgan slowly. 'It's not quite as simple as that. I was wondering if — '

'What more do you want?' snapped Brad sharply. He was beginning to smell a rat.

It was a very large and dangerous animal.

The Power Guild held a monopoly of geigers and, without them, it would be suicide to attempt to enter the radioactive areas. Scavengers could take a chance if they wanted to but, before their salvaged goods could be offered for sale, each item had to be checked by guildsmen and sealed with their warrant of safety.

Morgan wanted to by-pass the Guild.

'You know all about atomics,' he whispered eagerly. 'You know all about the safe levels of radiation. You can make and read geigers. Man! You've got it made!'

Brad didn't comment.

'Listen,' continued Morgan. 'You can guide us to the safe areas. You know where the rich stuff is to be found. You can even tell us how long we can work in the hot places. I'll fit out an expedition and we'll go in and clean up. We'll cut out the Guild and make a fortune.'

'What about the Guild seal?'

Morgan shrugged.

'Forged?' Brad nodded. 'It would have to be.'

'What's in a forged seal? With you checking out the stuff there's nothing to go wrong. No one's going to complain. No one's going to get hurt. I don't want to sell hot goods but if we cut out the Guild we'll double the profit. Hell, what are you worried about? One successful trip and you'll be made.'

'Or in jail.'

'Jail?'

'Places where they put people who've broken the law,' said Brad dryly. Maybe he didn't mean jail but one thing was certain — if he was caught he would suffer. The Guild would protect its own.

Thoughtfully he stared down into the city. Khan was behind this, of course, that was obvious. He had set up the rendezvous and he had been smooth about it. There was nothing to connect him to the scavenger but his very caution warned Brad of danger.

'Well?'

Morgan was impatient. He rested his hand above Brad's elbow and his fingers were like steel. Brad had the impression that, if he refused, the scavenger would throw him over the edge. He looked over his shoulder.

'The guard's watching us.'

'Never mind him — what's your answer?'

'Let go my arm.' Brad waited, stepped a couple of feet away. Morgan wouldn't murder before witnesses — but a man could always fall. 'Thanks but — no thanks.'

'What — ?'

'You heard what I said. The idea's crazy. Forget it.'

'You're a fool, Stevens. There's an easy fortune to be made.'

'Maybe, but I'm not interested in anything illegal.'

'You moral bastard,' said Morgan. Above the beard his face was white, the eyes wild. 'It's all right for you to sponge on a man with a soft head but when it comes to getting down to earning a living you get choosey. Who the hell are you to preach to me?'

'You'd better go,' said Brad.

'I'll go.' Morgan's hands were clenched, his voice a sneer. 'I can't stand the stink of you parasites. You make me sick, the lot of you. Go to hell, you sponging creep!'

He stalked off, an indignant man.

5

The dancers were nude, their oiled bodies gleaming in the spotlight, writhing in uninhibited abandon to the pulsing rhythm of drums. The dance ended. Like waves pounding a shore applause rose from the audience.

'Did you like it?' Serge leaned across the table, eyes bright in the subdued illumination. Helen nodded.

'They were superb.'

'They should be. Aktin danced at the temple of Apollo and the girl was a high priestess of Baal.' He caught her smile. 'You don't believe them?'

'Do I have to?'

'No. But — '

'Listen, Serge. In my time the difference between publicity and outright lying was so small that it didn't exist. You mustn't blame me for not believing everything I hear. In any case, does it matter? Their dancing was still superb.'

'Yes,' he said, and hesitated. 'Well, never mind. Let's have another drink.'

It was a thick, green, oily liqueur with an odd saline flavour distilled, she knew, from a species of mutated seaweed farmed in the estuary gardens. It was both strong and expensive. She caught his arm as he turned again to the waiter.

'No more for me, Serge.'

'You must, this is a celebration.' He waited until they had fresh drinks. 'I saw Colman today. He was impressed with your sketches and you're going to hear from him soon. I didn't want to say anything until you had but — '

'I'd never have forgiven you!' She looked at him, her eyes shining. 'Serge! This is wonderful!'

'It's a beginning. Tell me, were all scientists fashion designers in your time?'

'Not unless they did it as a hobby. I used to design clothes for dolls and sometimes for myself and friends.' She smiled. 'I even toyed with the idea of becoming a model but they told me that I was too fat.'

'Well built,' he corrected. 'Very well built.'

'You flatter me.'

'Truth is never flattery.'

'Thank you for the compliment.' She became serious. 'When Colman calls how should I handle things?'

'The usual way. He will probably offer you a percentage deal based on the actual sale of your designs but I suggest that you ask for an immediate down-payment in cash and a lower percentage. And don't tie yourself to a long-term contract.'

'Should I contact a lawyer?'

'An adviser? I don't think it would do any real good. Colman's a fair dealer and prefers to work direct. I doubt if you would cover an adviser's fee by added advantage if you called one in — and you might alienate Colman.'

'I understand.' Impulsively she gripped his arm. 'Serge. I don't know how to thank you.'

'You don't have to.'

'I know different.' She took a deep breath. 'One day, perhaps, I'll be able to repay you.'

'Don't worry about it.'

'I can't help it. We've sponged off you

for long enough. I know that Brad is worried sick about it and I've felt the same way. Now — '

She broke off, staring across the room. A man weaved through the tables, brushing aside waiters, laughing with drunken exhilaration. Carl Holden was enjoying himself.

★   ★   ★

He was not alone. The woman with him looked like the Hollywood conception of a Babylonian princess and she moved with all the arrogant assurance of wealth.

'Velda,' said Serge quietly. 'One of Delancy's people.'

'You know her?'

'I know of her.' Serge frowned his distaste. Helen was curious.

'She looks very young and lovely.'

'She's neither.' He was very curt. 'She's a painted trollop almost eighty years old.'

'I don't believe it!'

'Why not?' He looked impatiently at his companion. 'Because she doesn't look her age? Well, why should she? With her share of the money she steers towards Delancy she can afford the best the Institute can offer in the way of cosmetic surgery and replacement grafts. That woman is a vampire and a ghoul.'

He sensed her bewilderment.

'I'm sorry. I forgot that you're still new to all this. You know that a shark is a moneylender?'

'Yes.'

'Well a vampire is someone who steers a gull, a potential borrower, into his clutches. A ghoul is someone who buys body-replacement parts.'

'From the Life Institute?'

'Usually, but not necessarily. They attend to the surgery and medication, of course, but they don't always have to supply the raw material from their body-banks. That's where Delancy comes in. He and his vampires like Velda.'

'I see.' Helen stirred the liquid in her glass. 'And a zombie? I heard the word somewhere,' she explained. 'Does it mean the same as it did in my time?'

'I don't know. What did it mean?'

'A zombie was one of the living dead.

Someone who had di~~ed~~ ~~ by~~
voodoo magic, had been res~~tored~~
kind of life so that the crea~~ture could~~
perform simple tasks.'

'It means much the same,' he said sho~~rtly.~~
He gestured to her drink. 'You'd bette~~r~~
finish that. You look as if you need it.'

'You could be right.' She emptied the
glass, not meeting his eyes. He looked at
her with sudden suspicion.

'Helen. Is anything wrong? Have you
been borrowing money?'

'No.'

'Are you sure?'

'I'm positive. I only have the hospital
debt.'

'The Institute? Well, that's bad enough,
but it can't be helped. But stay away
from the sharks. They have no mercy.
You start small, get scared or careless
and, before you know it, you're in over
your head. Don't ever borrow money,
Helen.'

'I won't. But Carl — '

'If you need anything come to me.' He
gripped her hand, forced her to look at
him. 'I want you to promise that.'

⌐ his concern. 'But

he is from my own
⌐e in trouble.' She
of the new clothes
⌐ldenly acquired, his
⌐onfidence, his irrespon-
sible ⌐ She had suspected that
he had becom⌐ the parasite of some rich
and jaded woman but now she wasn't so
sure. 'Do you know what he's up to,
Serge?'

'Carl? No.'

'Could you find out?'

'Perhaps, but is it important?' Serge
had little respect for the man. 'Even if I
did find out that he's acting the fool it
would serve no purpose. I couldn't stop
him. His life is his own.'

'Please, Serge. For me.'

He crushed a sudden jealousy. Her
concern for Carl was not emotional — it
was a leftover from the social conscience
of her time. He found it hard to
understand but knew that it was dangerous. It was something she would be wise

to be rid of. He thought he knew how it could be done.

★ ★ ★

Unpleasant things have a tendency to be hidden and so the Nightfair took place in the dark hours. It wasn't illegal, it wasn't even immoral, it was cold, merciless business and a part of the fabric of this society. But it dealt with things best forgotten and so, like the prisons, mental hospitals and workhouses of her own time, it was not thrust into public view.

Helen didn't like it.

She sat beside Serge on a long bench facing a raised dais in a hangar-like shed on the river-edge of the city. A car had carried them from the restaurant and Serge had been very silent. Now she knew why. For an hour she had sat and listened, watched and — was beginning to understand.

'Lot 32.' The auctioneer — Helen couldn't help but think of him as that — sat at a small desk, an elderly man with a mane of white hair and benign smile. 'Male. 32. Construction worker. Has had some experience in carpentry. Owes 1552 imperials to the Life Institute. What am I bid?'

'Must be something wrong with him,' said a voice to her rear. 'At that price they wouldn't be selling his debt unless he was unusable.'

'Sick, maybe,' echoed his partner. Helen had seen him, a fat, jolly man. 'One thing's for sure — there can't be much chance of his working off that debt in any reasonable time. Think we should bid?'

'Wait until we see him. Uh! I guessed there was something wrong.'

An attendant led a man to the dais. He was in apparent good health but he stumbled as he walked and would have fallen but for the attendant's hand.

'Diseased!' breathed the fat man. 'Ear canals gone so that he's lost his sense of balance. Incurable too, if the Institute are washing their hands of him. Tough.'

'As you can see the item has a physical disability of an incurable nature,' said the auctioneer. 'A full medical report is available. However, aside from the disability, he is in perfect health. What am I bid?'

'What good is a man like that?' whispered Helen to Serge. 'He can't walk unaided. He must feel constant nausea. Why don't they just put him to bed and keep him there?'

'Who will pay for his keep?'

'His relatives. Or — '

'He has no relatives willing to take the responsibility. His debt was incurred in trying to cure his disability. It can't be cured. He has no money and no hope of earning any. What else could the Institute do but to try and get something back by selling his debt?'

'You mean that I, or anyone, could just go up and buy him?'

'Yes — if the Institute accepted your offer.'

'And then?'

'Then his debt is yours. You can try to regain it the best you can. Put him to work of some kind. Hire him out. Sell him if you want to.'

'Sell him,' she said slowly. She felt a little sick. Things were beginning to fall into place, the sharks, vampires, ghouls — how did they get their replacement body-parts? During the past hour she had found the answer. 'I want to go,' she said.

'Not yet.'

'But, Serge — '

'I want you to watch this,' he said harshly. 'I want you to understand the risk you run when you borrow money you haven't got. This is the way we settle our debts.'

'This — slavery!'

'It isn't slavery,' he said patiently. 'A man can buy himself free any time he has the money to pay his debts. Or his debts can be paid for him. He must be allowed to remain a free agent and be given time in which to pay. Every contract has a time-clause. Every debt can be paid in instalments. Every effort is usually made to give a debtor every chance to clear himself. Is that slavery?'

'You said 'usually',' she pointed out. 'Suppose that I didn't want to give a debtor any chance of paying. What then?'

'Then, if the time-clause had run out, he'd be yours to dispose of.'

'Dispose of.' She swallowed, the smell of the place, though imaginary, was closing around her. 'You mean sell as spare parts to the body-banks? Is that what you're trying to tell me?'

'Yes.' He turned and looked at her, his eyes hard. 'If you borrow money then you must be prepared to pay it back. If you can't then you must accept that your creditor has the right to regain his money. If he has to sell your body to get it that's his right.'

Helen was suddenly very glad that she had the promise of financial security.

★　★　★

The flat was empty but Brad wasn't surprised. Carl was constantly out and Helen was probably off somewhere with Serge. He hoped that she was enjoying herself. He was not.

Morosely he switched on the radio. A female voice cooed at him with saccharine sweetness as he entered the bathroom.

'Worried? Depressed? Don't know which way to turn? Let the Delancy Trust take care of your financial woes. Big loans. Long periods. Personal attention. Drop in and see us at any time. Day and night service.'

A bell, a tune, a singing commercial. One thing, at least, hadn't changed.

The roar of the shower cut off the next commercial. Brad stepped under the hot spray, wincing as he soaped his body, frowning at the grime beneath his broken nails. For the past week he had worked as a labourer, hauling sewage to the docks for the estuary farms, and he wasn't used to the labour. Not that it mattered now. He'd been fired for inefficiency.

He lathered his hair and tilted up his face so as to keep the soap from his eyes, uncomfortably aware of the ache of overstrained muscles. He was even more uncomfortably aware of his inadequacy. An atomic physicist unable to hold down a labourer's job. So much for education.

Washed, he turned the shower to cold and shivered beneath the impact of the needle jets. Stepping out he grabbed a towel and rasped the rough fabric over his body until he was warm. Distastefully he looked at his soiled clothing then picked it up. Brushing it down, he donned his only suit. The female voice greeted him as he approached the radio.

'Want work? We have it. The Apex Agency. Low fees. Guaranteed situations. Personal attention.'

Brad swore, tuned to another station, swore again as an even, official voice read out a list of news items. Killing the radio he stared broodingly at the heap of books beside his drawing board. If muscle couldn't help him then intelligence must, but he had the uneasy feeling that he was wasting his time.

Tiredly he settled down to work.

The door chimed.

He frowned at it, wondering if it were Carl, drunk again and unable to use his key. Well, let him wait. Grimly he concentrated on his work.

The door chimed again.

'Go to hell,' he snapped. 'You've got a key — use it.'

The chimes sounded for a third time.

'Damn!' Brad glared at the panel, knowing that he couldn't ignore the summons. Irritably he jerked to his feet and snatched it open.

A man stood outside. A stranger, with a dirk.

6

He was dressed in the full regalia of a Highlander with plaid, kilt, claymore and skean dhu. His bonnet was bright with a feathered cockade. His brooches were of hammered silver. His face was smooth, dark, secretive. He spoke with a soft burr.

'You'll be Stevens?'

'That's right.' Brad kept his eyes on the dirk. It was a heavy, viciously efficient looking weapon. The stranger held it with an easy familiarity. The light gleamed from the blade as he hefted the dagger.

'A dirk makes a bonny key for a stubborn door,' he said. 'I'd a mind that maybe your chime wasna working as it should.'

'You'd have forced the door?'

'I'd no mind to bruise my knuckles without reason.' The stranger sheathed the weapon. 'I'm Jamie Macdonald of

Inverness down with a cargo of meat, hides and whisky for trade. I've been wanting words with you, Brad Stevens. Will you not be asking me inside?'

Brad hesitated, then stepped back, closing the door after his visitor. Macdonald stared about the room, his eyes sharp.

'Are you alone?'

'At the moment. I'm expecting Carl back at any time.'

'Holden? Och, man, that cull will no' be back this night.' He smiled at Brad's expression. 'And neither will the girl — not until we've had our talk.'

'You seem very sure of yourself.'

'I am. What I have to say to you canna be said before others.' Macdonald halted beside the drawing board. He frowned at what he saw. 'Yours?'

'Yes.'

'What is it?'

'Something I've been working on.' Brad looked down at the drawing board. He had seen better plans but he was not a professional draughtsman. 'Something I hope to sell.'

'What is it?'

'That's my business.'

'Aye,' Macdonald didn't seem to be offended. 'So it is.' Idly he reached forward and lifted a few sheets. He raised his eyebrows. 'Maps?'

'Of London as I remember it.' Brad leaned forward to cover the drawings. Casually the Scot thrust him to one side. His strength was irresistible. He looked again at the top sheet.

'What's a laser beam?'

Brad didn't answer. Inwardly he cursed himself for having labelled his work so boldly.

'I asked a question,' said Macdonald softly. 'I wouldna like it if I had to ask it again.'

'It's an electronic machine capable of delivering a beam of energy which can be used for communication or construction.' Brad shrugged. 'You could call it a kind of heat ray.'

'A weapon?'

'It could be used as that.'

'And you could make one?'

'If I had the materials and equipment, yes.'

'And other things? Geigers so that we could find our way into the safe areas?'

'Yes,' said Brad shortly. He could guess what was coming.

He hoped that it wouldn't take too long.

★　★　★

There were politics in this world as there had been in every world. As there would probably be until the end of time. Politics and ambition and rebellion against the order of things.

Macdonald was a rebel.

'I'll give it to you straight, Stevens,' he said. 'We need you up north. The Laird will make a place for you, give you what you need, treat you with respect. You'll have rank and riches and men to do your bidding. Not many Sassenachs are offered as much.'

Brad wasn't impressed. The Highlands had escaped most of the damage but Scotland had been sparsely populated, the land almost valueless, the old way of life destroyed long before the Débâcle.

With the industrial cities gone only a barren wilderness had been left. Even now, with the clan-system once more come into its own, things could not begin to equal what could be found in the south. Macdonald sensed his thoughts.

'I'll not have you thinking that we're savages,' he said. 'We've a university and a love of learning. There's trade along the coast and with the south. Our ships reach Ireland and touch the Continent. We — '

'You live on cattle, cloth and whisky,' interrupted Brad. 'Your clan-system is strictly feudal. You've no decent road-network, no accessible minerals, little loot for easy picking. You're poor, Macdonald. You've always been poor.'

'Aye. And whose fault is that?'

'Not yours. The land and climate are against you. History finished what little chance you had. Maybe you've managed to rebuild the old way of life but it was never good. Crofters scratching a living and starving while their lairds lorded it in barbaric splendour. And what splendour was that? Against the petty nobles of the south they looked like poor relations.

Don't tell me things have altered that much!'

'No,' said Macdonald thickly. 'They haven't changed that much — but they could.'

'How? By hiring me to make a bomb so that you could wave it at the world? Haven't you had enough of that sort of thing?'

'Aye! Enough and more than enough!' Macdonald paced the floor with long strides, the knuckles of his left hand white as he gripped the basket hilt of his claymore. 'Mon, ye wrong me!'

Brad's shrug was cynical. Macdonald's eyes blazed with fury. With an effort he controlled himself.

'Och, I didna come to argue. Ye ken the Highlands?'

'I knew of them,' said Brad. He gestured towards the pile of books. 'I've been trying to catch up on recent history.'

'You'll no find much aboot the Highlands in books but ye'll ken the situation.'

'Aye,' said Brad dryly. 'I ken.'

It was the old story. The Power Guild

controlled all sources of power and without it the Highlands could never lift themselves from their horse-and-candle economy. Power was expensive because the installations weren't cheap and because the investment had to show a profit. The Highlands simply didn't have the money to expand. It was a vicious circle. Without money they couldn't buy the power to make money to buy the power. Brad could break the deadlock.

'We've the men and the will but we haven't the knowledge,' said Macdonald. His brogue had lessened with the diminishing of his temper. 'You have. With you to guide us we can break the power of the Guild. We'll be independent of them. We can even probe south to the cities for loot. Man! You've got to agree!'

'No.'

'But I've explained how much we need you. Surely you can see that?'

Macdonald sounded a little desperate. Brad wasn't impressed.

'I can see it,' he said. 'But I don't have

to agree. Not now. Not yet. I'd want to think about it first.'

'Aye.' Macdonald visibly relaxed. 'My ship will be here a while yet, you've time enough to think.' He hesitated by the door. 'But think hard, man. Up north you'll be treated like a king. Consider it.'

'I will,' said Brad. 'Good night.'

'Good night.'

Alone Brad sat and thought about it. The challenge was exciting but he had no illusions. Macdonald was sincere but he had a different set of values. In the feudal society of the Highlands Brad would be little better than a gilded slave helpless to do other than obey.

But would it be so very different to his present position?

He sighed and rummaged through his pockets. His pay made a small heap of crumpled notes and coins. Enough, perhaps, to starve on for another week. Not enough to buy a suit. Nowhere near enough to begin paying off his debts.

It was time he stopped being cautious.

*   *   *

The dice were dancing cubes of ivory on a sea of emerald green.

'Four,' droned the croupier. 'The point is four.'

Brad watched as the player snatched up the cubes, shaking them, whispering to them in the age-old prayer of those who sought to beat the gods of chance.

'Come on, baby, give me that four. Roll right for daddy. Roll right down the green and show that four. Come on now and — '

Four. Six sides to a dice — six to one against any one number showing. Two cubes — thirty-six to one against any specific combination. The dice were matched — halve the odds. Eighteen to one against the player getting two twos — nine to one against him getting his four.

Six to one against him getting a seven — and out.

The odds were in favour of the house.

'One imperial against the player.' Brad dropped a note. A fat man covered it. They waited as the dice skittered down the cloth.

'Six — the point is four.'

'Again.

'Five — the point is four.'

'Again.'

'Four — the hard way. The player wins.'

Brad watched his money being swept away. Again he calculated the odds and made his bet. Again he lost. He bet again and won. And won. And lost. And won.

An hour later he left the table. He had lost half his money and learned that luck still defied the laws of mathematical probability. Figuring the odds simply wasn't good enough.

Unless he could cut down the odds.

He halted beside a roulette layout. The game hadn't altered. The same wheel, the same ball, the same system of betting. Red and black paid evens, but he knew that, no matter what the sequence, each colour had exactly the same chance of coming up at each turn of the wheel. The trick was to predict what it would be.

He was a lousy predictor. Fifteen minutes later he was down to his last imperial and had learned another lesson.

A man who cannot afford to lose never wins.

So?

So find a man who has got to win — and bet against him.

It was a policy of desperation but the only one he had. Grimly he surveyed the players at the table. A matron with jewels, a young escort and a heap of chips. She was backing numbers — no good. A scatter of casual players. An elderly man who stacked his chips with bored indifference. A thin, hot-eyed man who looked like a low-paid clerk and who watched each spin of the wheel with febrile eyes.

Brad concentrated on the thin man.

He'd been backing numbers, extending his bets to cover a wider field at lower odds. Now, with a gulp, he put money on the black.

Brad backed the red.

Red won.

The thin man put more money on the black. Brad picked up his winnings leaving his original stake on the red. He regretted it as the ball bounced to a stop.

Red won. The thin man switched to red. Brad switched his money to the black.

Black won.

Three wins in a row. Brad drew a deep breath, fighting the dangerous feeling of euphoria at having beaten the system, the desire to plunge and ride the winning streak. His own luck wasn't good — he was cashing in on the fact that the thin man's luck was bad.

The next spin was zero — they both lost. The next three showed two wins for Brad, one for the thin man. In the next half hour Brad had doubled the money he'd brought with him.

Then the thin man ran out of cash.

He rose from the table, his face grey, his eyes sick with inner hurt. He stumbled a little as he crossed the room and stood for a while against a wall, head resting on the cool surface. No one paid him any attention. No one but Brad and a guard.

The guard was a quiet man dressed in inconspicuous grey, the colour of the walls. His hand rested easily above the butt of his gun. He sensed Brad beside him and nodded towards the thin man.

'He a friend of yours?'

'No. Is he all right? He looks ill.'

'He's a loser,' said the guard. 'I've had my eye on him. If you ask me he's hit rock-bottom.' He drew in his breath with a soft, moist sound. 'I just hope that he doesn't cause trouble.'

'Trouble? What could he do?'

'A lot of things. A guy like that can burn his loop. Maybe he's got a gun under his coat and the yen to hit back. I knew a guy once who came in here with a belt of dynamite all ready to blow the lot if he lost. I got that one just in time.'

'You killed him?'

'Not me. I broke his arms with a couple of slugs before he could torch the fuse. A near thing, though. I sure earned that bonus.' The guard tensed as the thin man straightened. He looked about him with blind, animal-eyes, then lurched towards the door. The guard relaxed as he reached the portal.

'O.K. He's out of my hair.'

'But he looks ill. He might do something stupid.'

'Mister,' said the guard casually. 'Once

he's out of here I don't give a damn.'

He relaxed against the wall, eyes scanning the players, not looking after Brad as he hurried from the room.

⋆ ⋆ ⋆

There was a stairway, a door, the opening to the street. A red sign painted the road with ruby light, touching the cheeks of pedestrians with garish colour. It was late and traffic was light. The thin man was a shadow standing at the kerb.

A guard, twin to the one above, watched him with stolid anticipation.

'This,' he said to Brad, 'is going to be good.'

The thin man held a gallon-sized can. He had probably collected it from the cloakroom downstairs — odd packages and mysterious parcels were not allowed into the upper precincts. As Brad watched he stooped, opened it, lifted it above his head.

The raw stench of spirit filled the air.

Deliberately the thin man emptied the contents over his head. Spirit drenched his hair, ran over his face, soaked into his clothing. A puddle of it formed around his feet. The can made a faint, metallic noise as he threw it to one side. Reaching into a pocket the man produced a box of matches.

'A flamer,' said the guard. He hadn't moved. None of the little crowd assembled around the thin man had moved. Instead they watched with ruby-tinted eyes, their faces eager with anticipation.

Waiting for the man to light the match and burn himself to death.

'No!' Brad stepped forward. 'You can't let him do it!'

'Why not?' The guard was genuinely bewildered. 'The guy's burning his loop. He wants out in his own way. Why should anyone stop him? He isn't threatening anyone else.'

Brad didn't answer. He lunged forward as the man scraped a match against the side of the box. He was lucky — the match didn't fire. Before he could try again Brad was on him, one hand slashing the matches from his grasp, the other shoving him away from the puddle on the floor.

'You fool!' he snapped. 'You stupid fool!'

'Damn you!' The thin man sobbed in his anger. 'Why did you have to interfere? Why did you have to spoil it?'

'Spoil it? I've just saved your life.'

'It's my life, you damned cripple. My life!'

He flung himself towards Brad, hands reaching for his throat. The stench of spirit was nauseating, it wet his hands, stung his eyes, clogged his breathing. Twice fingernails almost reached his eyes. Once a knee almost ground into his groin. Brad realized that he was fighting a maniac. Coldly he drew back his fist, slammed it hard to the jaw. He let the limp body fall.

'All right,' he said tiredly. 'Maybe you can take care of him. Call an ambulance or something. The guy's crazy.'

Nobody answered. They stood in a tight circle, the light from the sign ugly on their faces. The guard let out his breath in a fretful sigh.

'A flamer,' he said. 'Right smack on the doorstep. And you had to go and spoil it.'

'That's right,' said a plump man. 'Why did you do it? Did he owe you money or something?'

'No.' Brad stepped away from the unconscious man. 'He didn't owe me money. I just didn't want to see him kill himself that way.'

'Why not?'

'What's it to you?'

'A man's got the right to burn his loop if he wants.'

'It's his life, isn't it?'

'Damn cripples! Always interfering!'

The comments rose in a whisper of hate. The crowd surged forward a little, crowding Brad back into the street. A car hummed past inches from his back.

'Now wait a minute! I don't understand. What's the matter with you people? You — '

He broke off as a match flamed and arced towards him. Frantically he moved to one side, stamping it out, suddenly cold with terror. Desperately he looked towards the entrance of the gambling house. If he could get inside the house-guard would protect him but there was no chance of that. The crowd barred his passage. Only the regular police could save him now — and he could see no police.

Only the mob as it closed around him.

7

Brad turned and ran, smashing aside those who had circled behind him, diving across the road, heedless of the shriek of brakes and the car which almost ran him down. He reached the other side of the road and began to run against the direction of traffic. He didn't choose his direction. A cluster of people on the other side of the road did it for him. He ran from them as they joined the original crowd.

He was running for his life.

He knew it with a cold detachment which had nothing to do with logic or sanity but operated on a strictly primitive level. Those behind him were hunters — he was their quarry. How and why didn't matter. If they caught him he would die. It was as simple as that.

And the odds were against him.

Not because he couldn't run as fast as those behind — desperation lent wings to his feet — but because others were joining in the chase. Those to either side. Those ahead. Everyone in the city, it seemed, had suddenly acquired a craving for his blood. The hysteria was contagious.

He jerked to a stop as a party emerged from a side street a few yards ahead. Again he dived across the road, gaining a little time as traffic barred immediate pursuit. Lights ahead told of a main road and he headed towards it, racing down an alley. A figure loomed before him and he struck out, feeling the jar of fist on bone, not caring if the man were innocent or intended harm. A yell led the pursuers after him.

His heart sank as he reached the main road. He had been outguessed and outraced. To either side the mob was waiting. Others faced him across the concrete. More followed down the alley. Their noise was terrifying.

Desperately he ran to a door, tested it, found it locked. Chest heaving he leaned against the panel, fighting the instinctive desire to run, knowing that, unless he had a plan, he would only run to his death.

Damn the police! Where were they?

His eyes searched the street. No police. No guards. Nothing but the gathering mob, taking its time now that they had him trapped. Hope sent his eyes to the building before which he stood. Perhaps he could climb to a point of refuge and wait until help came. The hope died as he examined the façade. Smooth stone and smoother glass. His head turned as a horn sounded down the street. It was not the police. It was a truck, big, ponderous, grinding steadily forward well away from the sidewalk.

A truck!

He tensed, weighing time and distance, knowing that this was his last chance to escape. The vehicle drew close and he lunged from the doorway, racing down and across the street in the same direction as the truck. The vehicle sounded its horn again, caught up with him, began to pass and, with a final explosion of energy, Brad flung himself at the vehicle.

His hands scrabbled, caught a rope, the jerk tearing at his shoulders. He lifted his feet, twisted, kicked at a snarling face. Hands clawed at him. A man repeated his manoeuvre only to fall as Brad drove his foot into his throat. He climbed higher on the roped load, praying that the driver wouldn't stop.

He didn't.

Behind him the mob brayed its baffled anger.

★   ★   ★

Brad rode the truck until his breathing eased and the cold sweat of fear had died from his body. He dropped off at an intersection when the vehicle slowed and looked at himself in a shop window. He was a mess. His jacket was a mass of tatters still reeking with the stench of spirit. He took it off and tossed it away. The night was warm enough for shirt and trousers and he didn't want to look a tramp. He checked his pockets — aside from a few coins his money was gone. His winnings had fallen from his pockets or been taken, it didn't matter which. He was alive — that was enough. Alive but lost.

The area seemed deserted but he wasn't worried. City born and bred he knew that he could find his way simply by heading towards the silhouettes of the high, central buildings or, if he found one, asking directions from a passer-by. Confidently he set out. It took him fifteen minutes to get completely disorientated.

He had tried a promising street which had somehow dwindled to a maze of alleys flanked by warehouses from which seeped entrancing odours together with the unmistakable scent of hot metal and burning oil. He frowned as he sniffed the air, wondering a little why the ground should be so broken underfoot.

He wondered, too, why the area should be so dark.

Something clinked behind him in the alley. A small sound as if a stone had turned beneath a foot or a metal accoutrement had signalled its presence. It was followed by a sibilant hiss as of indrawn breath or of clothes brushing against a wall.

Brad ran.

He raced down the alley, springing high

into the air to avoid obstructions, eyes wide as they strained into the darkness. Behind him came a muffled oath and the sound of heavy feet in pursuit.

'Gut me, Tom,' rasped a savage voice. 'Ye've let 'im take wing. Why didn't ye down 'im wi' yer barkers?'

'Stow yer gab,' wheezed a heavy reply. ' 'Tis yer own fault yer clumsy-footed oaf. The cull — '

The voice dissolved into foul obscenities as the speaker stumbled and Brad, running at full speed, darted around a corner and felt a sudden relief as he saw a splotch of yellow light ahead.

It came from a smoking torch jutting from an ornamented bracket of wrought-iron mounted on the wall above a dark opening beneath. The ground before it was rough, unpaved, slimed with wet mud. Brad made squelching noises as he ran towards the light. A man stepped from the door as he approached.

He was tall, thin, dressed in the long waistcoat and high boots popular among highwaymen of the eighteenth century. His hair was long and clubbed with a ribbon. A rapier hung from a baldrick suspended from one shoulder. A ring gleamed on the hand he rested on its hilt.

He wasn't alone. Others crowded behind him, some with high powdered wigs and frogged coats, some with grimed faces and stained aprons, a few exquisites sniffing disdainfully at scented handkerchiefs of delicate lace. All stared at Brad with the peculiarly hungry expressions of men bored and eager for any distraction.

'Hold hard, my bucko!' The highwayman swaggered forward, drawing his rapier with a hiss of steel, aiming the point at Brad's eyes. 'Now, sir,' he demanded. 'What brings you to Alsatia?'

Brad felt himself tense. He knew of Alsatia, the modern facsimile of that infamous area of old London which had been the sanctuary of thieves, footpads and murderers. He knew something else. In the facsimiles there was no official law other than the Great Edict. A man entered them at his own risk.

'Well?' The rapier advanced an inch towards his eyes.

'Swounds!' drawled one of the exquisites. 'The clod has but little conversation. Give him a prick or two, Jack. Mayhap 'twill loosen his tongue.'

'Aye, Lord Cecil,' grinned the highwayman. 'There's naught like a touch of cold steel to open a sealed trap.'

He made a sudden thrust which would have blinded an eye had the point reached its target, but Brad had made his decision. He couldn't run. He couldn't hope to appeal for help and the odds were against his fighting. He could only pretend. Disdainfully he parried the blade with a sweep of his arm.

''Sdeath!' he roared in what he hoped was an acceptable accent. 'Am I a cull to be so treated? Is Dick Turpin not worthy of a warmer welcome?' He swaggered towards the doorway. 'Stand aside, dogs, and let your better sink his face in a stoup of ale!'

Incredibly it worked but there was no reason why it shouldn't. Aside from his clothing there was nothing to differentiate Brad from a true retro and, as long as he stayed in character, he was in little immediate danger. But the danger was still present. He sensed it as he thrust himself through the door and into Alsatia. He was a stranger, oddly dressed and unknown to those present. Like a pack of wild dogs they would turn against him at his first mistake.

And there were so many ways he could make an error.

He had never been inside Alsatia and had never seen a plan of the original, but the highwayman he claimed to be would have known it well. And the facsimile was modelled on the memories of those who had lived in the past. So he should know the way to the tavern, the lodging houses, the stews. And he was suddenly very conscious of eyes watching and waiting to see what he would do.

'This way, Dick,' whispered a voice at his side. A small, dirty creature with a shock of red hair and a patch over one eye jerked his head in an almost impercep- tible gesture. 'Ye'll be heading for Maloney's Tavern for that stoup of ale?'

'Aye,' rasped Brad. 'Do you go ahead and order a firkin of the best. Dick

Turpin's not a man to see his friends thirst when he has rhino in his pocket.'

He jingled his few coins as he spoke and hoped they would be enough to pay for the ordered ale. A firkin, he thought, was a small barrel, or was it a big one? He shrugged. His memory in such matters was slight and now he could only trust to luck. Luck and the small man, who called himself John Clutterbuck, now running down a narrow alley lined with squat houses heavy with wooden beams.

Maloney's Tavern was a long, smoke-filled place with an open fire and a clutter of wooden tables and benches scattered on the packed dirt of the floor. Serving wenches, painted, buxom, bare-shouldered trollops carried immense jacks of ale from the quarters at the rear, the prettier ones holding bottles of wine as they waited on the gentry lounging in carefully cultivated boredom on the settles to each side of the fire.

Maloney himself, a barrel of a man wrapped in a thick, leather apron, greeted Brad as he entered the tavern. A fist like a ham engulfed his own as the huge innkeeper roared a welcome.

'Indeed and 'tis good to see ye, Dick. There's many of the profession who'll be none too pleased to see a new star in the sky.' A prodigious wink accompanied the words. 'But I take it ill that ye've kept me waiting so long? D'ye mind the time when ye and Frank and — '

Clutterbuck, scuttling like a rat beside the taverner, plumped himself down and rapped his mug on the table.

'Less o' the gab and more of the ale,' he snapped. 'Fall in, lads. Dick's treat!'

They needed no second invitation. The scum of the streets seemed to have gotten wind of the free drinks and they clustered around, gulping down the brew and filling the room with noise. Brad was glad to join them. The innkeeper had too many memories for his liking. Clutterbuck had interrupted just in time.

The ale was nothing like what he had expected. It was dark, wet and, he supposed, strong but that was about all. He wondered where these people found hops and grain for their ale. Perhaps they couldn't and had to make do with substitutes. Much of every facsimile would have to be synthetic, no matter what age it represented. Each would have to be a matter of compromise.

Such as this tavern and the gentry lounging beside the fire. That was wrong. Gentry, in such a place and time, would have had their own rooms far from the noise and vulgarity of the ordinary taprooms. But Alsatia was small and there could be neither money nor labour to rebuild the London these people had known.

Brad sighed and sipped his ale, forcing his mind from theoretical considerations to more immediate necessities. At the moment he was safe but it was a temporary safety and he still had to get out of Alsatia and back to a more familiar world.

He felt a tug at his arm. Clutterbuck stared at him, an odd expression in his single, uncovered eye.

'Is something amiss, Dick? The ale not to your liking, mayhap?'

'Nay, 'tis naught.'

'There's a buxom wench I know of

who'll smooth the crease from your brow.' The suggestion in the small man's voice was unmistakable. 'She's a prime partner for rogering, Dick.'

'Nay.' Hastily Brad changed the subject. Looking up he caught a glare of hate from the highwayman who had met him at the gate. 'What's amiss with him?'

'Jack Murrey?' Clutterbuck shrugged. 'He's a vain coxcomb and likes not to be shamed. You put him in bad odour with my Lord Cecil there at the portal.'

'When I knocked aside his sword?' Brad shrugged. 'He was lucky that I didn't shove it down his throat.'

'Mayhap 'twould have been — ' Clutterbuck broke off as Murrey thrust himself forward. His face was flushed, his eyes murderous, ale slopped from the tankard in his hand.

'So, my brave bucko,' he sneered at Brad. 'My Lord Cecil's much taken with your manner. His words to me were not as smooth as of wont.'

'So?'

'So mayhap 'tis time to crop your comb. But I'm a fair-minded man with all who love life. Admit now, to these present, that I'm the better man and the matter's closed.'

Brad heard the suck of breath close to his shoulder. In the silence Clutterbuck's whisper sounded very loud.

'Tread warily, Dick,' he breathed. 'Jack's a bitter man when in his cups.'

It was a warning Brad had to ignore. It was essential to stay in character and Dick Turpin, the infamous highwayman, would never have run from such a quarrel.

'Go to hell!' he snapped.

Without preamble Murrey flung the contents of his tankard directly towards Brad's face. Expecting the gesture he ducked, flung aside the table as he straightened and hit Murrey flush on the mouth.

In such a place, among such people, the rest was inevitable.

The preparations were few. Benches and tables were cleared so as to leave a space clear for the duellists. Murrey, aided by his cronies, stripped himself to ruffled shirt, trousers and boots. Clutter-buck, appointing himself Brad's second, hunted through the company until he managed to borrow a sword.

It was much heavier than the *épée* which had been Brad's favourite weapon, but it had a point, blade and hilt and he had no doubt that he could handle it.

'I'll wager a hundred on Murrey,' drawled one of the gentry. 'A hundred against a score, markee. First blood to settle.'

'Nay, Charles,' protested one of his friends. 'Cut not the sport so short. The first two of three.'

'A pox on your caution!' shouted a fat, florid man, his face mottled beneath a powdered peruke. ' 'Tis a fair fight and so let it be to the death!'

The roar that echoed his words reminded Brad of the mob. These people wanted the vicarious thrill of seeing a man die and, from his expression, Murrey intended to give it to them.

' 'Ware his tricks,' breathed Clutterbuck as he stood at Brad's side. 'Trust him least when he seems to be off his guard.'

'I'll watch it.' Brad hefted the weapon, adjusting his grip on the hilt. 'If you want to pick up some easy money take the bets that are flying around. On me. I'm going to walk away from this.'

Brad saw the single eye narrow and, too late, remembered what he was supposed to be. Well, it couldn't be helped. God alone knew how the genuine Turpin would have phrased the suggestion and he had more important things to concentrate on than the correct accent. His life, for example. Murrey wanted it.

He came in with a cat-like slither of feet, his body crouched and balanced by his left arm. It was not the accepted fencer's posture but he was not using the accepted fencer's weapon and Brad did not make the mistake of underestimating his skill.

Brad fell into the familiar stance, automatically taking guard in the sixth position, the blades touching with a faint, metallic click oddly loud in the hushed silence of the tavern.

It was a hush that would not last for very long. Duels, by their nature, are short, sharp and vicious. When one man is out to kill another he does not waste time and, if he is fighting with swords, he dare not. The sheer, physical exertion of wielding a heavy length of metal held in an awkward position precludes the luxury of delay.

But Murrey was enjoying himself. He was performing before friends. He wanted to enhance his reputation and underestimated his opponent.

He intended to kill Brad — slowly.

He disengaged, feinted a lunge, withdrew on guard. He disengaged and repeated the manoeuvre. Brad wondered if he thought he was fooling anyone.

'Now ye scut!' snarled Murrey. 'I'll prick yer right shoulder.'

His blade disengaged, feinted but, instead of withdrawing, he continued the attack with a one two. Brad casually snapped his blade into fourth, back to sixth, into fourth again and riposted with a lunge to the announced target. Murrey, livid with rage, sprang back, a spot of red marring the whiteness of his shirt on the right shoulder.

'First blood to Dick!' yelled Clutterbuck.

' 'Twas a fluke,' snapped the florid man. 'A lucky hit, no more.'

Brad paid no attention to the comment. He knew, and Murrey should have known, that he could have killed as easily as wounding during that exchange, but it was a thing the highwayman refused to accept.

'God rot me,' he snarled. 'Let there be an end to this play-acting!'

He came in with a disengage, counter disengage, the blades circling in gleaming brilliance as Brad parried. He did not riposte. Unlike Murrey he had no intention of killing. He was content to wait on the defensive, allowing the other to tire himself out, and then either to wound or disarm.

But he had forgotten his fighting instincts developed during long hours of arduous training. To parry meant to riposte in a smooth burst of action which required no conscious effort or decision. To win a bout you had to hit before being hit and do it quickly. As Murrey attacked again, this time with more caution, Brad's trained reflexes took over.

He parried, counter-parried and then, blades circling, made a progressive time-attack in counter-sixth. Even then he had no intention of killing. But the point was sharp, the sword heavy and Murrey had been lunging forward.

The blade slid between his ribs and transfixed his heart.

8

' 'Twas a fine fight,' gloated Clutterbuck. 'Neat, quick, clean. Ye be a fine swordsman, Dick. 'Tis the best piece of work I've seen for many a day.'

He jingled a bag of coins and grinned at Brad. Around them the company swilled the free ale the little man had provided in celebration. Murrey had been dragged away, the floor swilled, the tables and benches returned to the centre of the room.

Life, in Alsatia, had returned to normal.

'I was just lucky.'

Brad didn't want to talk about it. He had curtly refused the offer of the dead man's clothing, his, as had been pointed out, by right, but had left such ghoulish rewards to those who had disposed of the body. He hadn't wanted to join the celebration but had been given little choice. Now, all he wanted to do, was to get out of this madhouse.

'Yes,' said Clutterbuck in a changed voice. 'You were lucky, Stevens, but your luck is just about to run out.'

'What?' Brad tensed with sudden alarm. 'What did you call me?'

'Sit down, you fool! Don't act startled. Don't raise your voice. Have some of that ale.'

Somehow the small man had changed. He looked the same but he was no longer the greasy pimp to whom Alsatia was a natural home.

'I recognized you at the gate,' he said quietly. 'It was lucky for you that I did. Do you know what retros do to a pretender?'

'No, but I can guess.'

'It isn't pleasant,' said Clutterbuck. 'In fact there's only one thing worse.' He buried his face in his tankard. 'Keep drinking. You've got to act the person you claim to be. You haven't done a very good job of it so far. Refusing those clothes was stupid.'

'Why?'

'You're supposed to be the notorious

highwayman Dick Turpin. He'd steal the washing from a line if he had the chance and wasn't choosey about wearing dead men's clothes. None of us are.'

'What do you know about Turpin?'

'More than you, apparently. I suppose it was the first name you could think of but it wasn't one to arouse much respect. Turpin was a coward most of the time, untrustworthy all of it. He ditched his friends and was hanged for horse stealing after getting into a stupid quarrel a moron would have avoided. He would never have fought Murrey. If he had he could never have beaten him. You stepped right out of character there and I think you've aroused suspicion.'

'So what?' Brad helped himself to more ale. 'They know better than to tangle with me.'

He took another sip of the ale. It had finally gone to his head and he felt a little muzzy and more than a little boastful. It was a dangerous feeling and, vaguely, it worried him.

'You're drunk,' said Clutterbuck dispassionately. 'Drunk or a fool and I don't think that you're a fool. Do you think they'll call you out as Murrey did? There are other ways of getting rid of a man.'

'Murder?' Brad shook his head to clear it of fumes. 'Murder is forbidden by the Great Edict.'

'Sure it is, but Jack had a lot of friends. They aren't going to let you get away with killing him. And murder is only prevented by the fear of punishment. Eliminate that fear and you'll be lucky to see another dawn.'

Brad knew that fear could be eliminated. He had known it while being chased by the mob. Murder was forbidden, which explained the guards in public places. No one, by intent or carelessness, was allowed to injure another if it could be prevented. But a mob was not an individual. A mob could not be punished.

And Alsatia had an ugly reputation for violence.

★　★　★

Clutterbuck chose the time. With Brad leaning heavily on his shoulder he lurched towards the door of the tavern.

'John, lad, be ye going so soon?' A villainous man leered from where he caressed a giggling serving wench.

'Dick's drained his last pot this night,' snickered the little man. He heaved Brad's arm higher over his shoulder. 'I doubt me not that Molly will be glad of company. Mayhap she'll remember the one who filled her bed.'

'Aye,' yelled a man. 'And mayhap Dick'll be wanting to fill ye wi' cold steel when he wakes and finds where he is.'

A roar of laughter followed them from the tavern. Not until they had reached the shelter of an alley did Clutterbuck allow Brad to straighten.

'Thanks,' he said. He drew deep breaths of the clean air. 'I'll be all right now.'

'You think so?' Clutterbuck pulled him deeper into the dancing shadows thrown by a guttering torch. 'Listen.'

From the tavern came a sudden gust of voices.

'To Molly's, lads. 'Tis a shame to spoil the wench her fun but I doubt me not that she'll enjoy what we have to offer as much.'

'I've a mind to see him flayed.'

'Aye, bucko. Flayed and singed over a slow fire. Jack was a good friend and I've no mind to see him unavenged.'

The voices died as men moved down the street away from where Brad was hiding. He touched his face and found it beaded with sweat. He felt sick. He should, he thought grimly, be getting used to mobs by now. Clutterbuck touched his arm.

'Time to go,' he whispered. He read Brad's expression. 'Molly will suffer naught but disturbed rest this night — and she'll mind that not at all.' He shook his head with annoyance. 'Damn this trick of speech! I get confused!'

It must, thought Brad, be difficult for him. The mental wrench of shifting from one existence to another must be hard. For a retro it was almost impossible. Yet, apparently, Clutterbuck had no real trouble.

Apparently?

Or was the little man, like himself, only a pretender?

'They'll be watching the gate,' he muttered. 'We'll have to scale the wall and dodge the bully boys outside. How are you feeling, Stevens? Head clear?'

Brad nodded.

'Good. Now follow me.'

Like a shadow the small man darted through a maze of narrow streets and twisting alleys. Twice he froze as a group of men, torches in hand, lumbered past. Brad guessed they were the same men who had left the tavern and he was thankful for his guide. Alone he would have lost his way in the warren of streets and fallen into their hands.

Clutterbuck paused. A door creaked open and a foetid smell of dirt, damp and mildew gushed from the opening. Gagging, he followed his guide, the tips of his fingers tracing a path along a rough wall. His foot rapped against the bottom of a staircase.

'Still!'

Brad could feel his companion's body stiffen as they crouched against the wall. Someone stirred in a room above. A mattress creaked beneath a heavy body. A snore echoed down the stairs and their tension relaxed.

'Up to the roof,' whispered Clutterbuck, his mouth touching Brad's ear. 'If anyone challenges you make sure they don't give the alarm! Understand?'

Brad nodded, his hands clenched into fists. Carefully they climbed the stairs.

'Now,' whispered the small man. 'I've got to climb on your shoulders. I'll be as fast as I can.' Like a monkey he swarmed upwards. Brad sagged beneath his weight.

'A moment. Uh — '

Wood creaked and an opening gaped above, a lighter patch in the darkness, and a stream of fresh air dispelled some of the fug. A solitary star, pale and wan, shone clear and then was occluded as Clutterbuck climbed through. He looked down, hand extended.

'Jump. Grab my hand and I'll pull you up.'

Brad bent his knees, jerked upwards, grabbed at the almost invisible hand. His fingers touched cloth, slipped over the wrist, failed to grip the hand. The crash of his fall echoed through the house.

'Quick!' Clutterbuck was frantic. 'Jump!'

This time Brad made it. He heard sinews crack as the little man heaved upwards, then his hands gripped the edge and he took over. Voices called from below as he lowered the skylight. Clutterbuck, astride the peak of the roof, looked back as he inched along.

'Hurry!'

He caught Brad at the far end, grabbing a chimney stack to support the weight, his single eye anxious as he stared into the other's face.

'Are you all right?'

Brad nodded, unable to speak, forcing himself to gulp lungfuls of air. Blindly he clutched at the chimney stack, at Clutterbuck.

'Acrophobia,' he finally managed to gasp. 'I've got a fear of heights.' A fear which hadn't been helped when he had lost balance and almost fallen.

'It isn't much farther,' urged the small man. 'Can you make it?'

'I'll make it.'

Together they crept towards the wall beyond which lay safety.

★ ★ ★

The street was wide and bright and clean with the scent of early dawn. Alsatia with its stink and vice, dirt and depravity, seemed very far away. An age away. Brad knew that he would never willingly go there again.

'That was close,' said Clutterbuck. He halted, his single eye gleaming as he looked at Brad. 'You look all in, Stevens.'

'The name's Brad.' He rubbed his aching forehead. Now that the danger was over the reaction was setting in. He was bruised, aching and his ankles hurt from the long drop from the wall. He felt that he needed a bath and a sleep. A hot bath and a long, long sleep.

But there was one thing he had to know.

'Who are you?'

'Does it matter?'

'It matters. I owe you my life and I'd like to know whom to thank.'

'You thanked me enough by winning that duel.' Clutterbuck grinned as he tapped his pockets. 'I won a stack because of that.'

'Money!'

'What's wrong with money?'

'Nothing,' said Brad shortly. In this cash-crazy world how could he talk of loyalty or rewards which couldn't be counted or thrust in a pocket. And yet something didn't add up. The little man hadn't helped him because of hope of gain. When he had won his money he could easily have left.

There was something odd about the man.

'Well,' said Clutterbuck. 'You can find your own way home from here, Brad. I'll be going.'

'Wait!'

Brad flung out a hand to catch him by the shoulder. He caught the shock of red hair instead. There was a soft, sucking sound. Brad stared at the wig in his hand.

'I see,' he said softly. 'The patch too?'

'Yes.'

'And the name?'

'That, at least, is genuine. Or was. I was known as Clutterbuck before starting this life as Grenmae.'

'Grenmae!' Brad thought he understood.

'Of course. You're a policeman. Serge has often spoken of you.'

'Nothing bad, I hope?'

He had stripped off the patch and wiped his face, the lines of dissipation vanishing with the paint. He straightened and he was no longer small. Slender and lithe but no longer small.

'No,' said Brad. 'Nothing bad. But — are you a retro?'

'A retro can't be a policeman,' said Grenmae evenly. 'And, in case you're wondering, I wasn't in Alsatia on official business. We don't worry about what goes on in facsimile.'

'Then — ?'

'What was I doing there?' Grenmae paused, smiling. 'I wonder if you could understand? Look. I was born and lived in old London of the mid-eighteenth century. It wasn't a happy existence. I was poor and you can probably imagine what that meant in those days. A poor man was literally dirt. I worked as an ostler, drawer, linkman, scavenger — anything which would provide bread. Most times I slept in the gutter. I couldn't read or write and never owned new clothes in my life. I had scabies, a hernia and rotten teeth. I had deformed legs from vitamin deficiency. I died beneath the wheels of a gentleman's carriage.'

'Grim,' said Brad.

'It was hell.' Grenmae was dispassionate. 'When I hear people talk of the romance of the past I want to spit. There was no romance — only dirt, ignorance and disease. I know. I was there. Yet still I visit Alsatia. Still I go back. Why? Can you tell me?'

'Yes,' said Brad. 'I can. You go back because you can quit any time you like. For you it's fun — because you don't have to stay. You're not going back to the old life. You visit Alsatia and talk the idiom and wear the clothes and imagine that you've stepped back in time. And you have, but a different time to what you remember. Now you're no longer poor, diseased, desperate. You can swagger like a lord or act the pimp or play the degenerate. But you don't have to sleep in the gutter or eat filth. There's always an escape.'

'And that's the answer?'

'Maybe not all of it — I wouldn't know. But this I do know. You can stand almost anything if, at any time, you can quit. It's when you can't quit that things become unbearable.'

'Are you sure about that, Brad?' Grenmae looked at the fading stars. 'Are you positive?'

'Yes.' Brad frowned, Grenmae was too intent. He wondered why. 'It's the difference between living in a barred cage from choice — or being confined to a cell for life. The environment is the same. The attitude is not. Or, to put it more simply, if you've got a key you don't have to beat your head against the door.'

'You can always walk out?'

'That's right.'

'And this, to you, is the difference between happiness and misery?'

'You could say that.' Brad's uneasiness grew. What had started to be a simple discussion was developing deep philosophical undertones. Grenmae smiled.

'You know, Brad, you're really talking about life.'

'I don't understand.'

'No? I was thinking of your analogy. The barred cage. That's life, isn't it? Some people imagine that they're stuck in it and can't get out. Others know that they can. At any time they wish. Which are you, Brad?'

'Does it matter?'

'It could. To you. It could matter quite a lot.' Grenmae shrugged. 'Well, never mind. I suppose we each of us know where we are as regards our attitude. Once I used to regard life as a prison. Now I don't. Maybe you — '

He broke off and shook his head.

'Well, never mind. But thanks for telling me why I visit Alsatia. You were right. You're no fool, Brad.'

'Thank you.'

'At least,' qualified Grenmae. 'I hope you're not a fool. Don't disappoint me now.' He smiled and waved and was on his way before Brad could answer.

Thoughtfully he stared after the man, wondering what he had been getting at. Grenmae was an odd type. But he wasn't a retro and there was no reason why he should be. Between those who could think of nothing but their earlier lives and those who didn't think about them at all must lie a broad spectrum of varying degree of involvement. But they all shared one thing in common.

They all dragged one foot in the past.

9

The water was cool, green, filled with mysterious shapes and graceful forms. Thick weed rose from the bottom, a forest of trailing tendrils in which lurked edible game. The scuba diver spotted a flash of silver. He halted, raised his harpoon gun, fired a barbed sliver of steel.

A graceful form gaped in the agony of death.

Carl Holden was having fun.

He wound in the line, gripped the fish in one hand and threshed his way to the surface. The sun was a blinding light from the protected waters of the estuary farm. A hand reached down from the raft and hauled him to the deck. He was laughing as he removed his mask.

'I got one!' he crowed. 'A real big one! Got him right smack in the gills!'

'Not bad.' Cyril Uwins, tall, handsome, dark-eyed and cynical, gave a mechanical smile as he examined the fish. It was a harmless thing, one of the stock-fish of the farm, edible but stupid and careless in its guarded waters. He wondered how Carl would react if he was ever faced with one of the mutated beasts lurking beyond the nets.

'Show me.' Velda, cunningly dressed in loose clothing which showed just enough to attract without spoiling the effect by over-exposure, strolled to where they sat. She stooped, her hair brushing Carl's cheek, one hand resting on his shoulder. He grinned at her with a smug sense of possession.

'Now if this were a bull,' he said. 'And I was a matador, I'd dedicate you its ears.'

'A fish has no ears,' said Cyril. He caught himself. 'But maybe you could dedicate its tail?'

'I'll do that. Has anyone got a knife?' He hesitated as Cyril passed him a blade. 'No. Wait. Maybe we'd better weigh it first. I want to win that bet.'

They weighed the fish. It was lighter than the one caught by Cyril. Carl frowned — he had lost too many bets lately.

'Never mind.' Cyril took both fish and threw them over the side. 'I'll tell you what. You try again and we'll take it from there. We know the weight of my catch. You beat it and we'll call it quits. If you don't then you owe me the hundred and you pay expenses.' He smiled at Carl's expression. 'Why look so glum? It's only money. And I'll tell you what — you catch two fish and we'll take the weight of the heaviest. Fair enough?'

It was more than fair. Velda caught Cyril's arm as Carl plunged over the side.

'Are you getting soft or something?'

'Don't be a fool.' He scowled at the thin trail of bubbles breaking the surface. 'I know the max weight of stock-fish and I know that slug of lead I loaded mine with lifts it way above. He hasn't got a chance. Not if he fishes all day.' He snorted a humourless laugh. 'How can anyone be so stupid?'

'It's just as well for us that he is.' Velda shivered a little in an off-sea breeze. 'Damn this outdoor life! What the hell you people find enjoyable in nature I'll never know. When are you going to hit him with the tab?'

'Soon. A week maybe.' He looked at the woman. 'I'll need more money.'

'You're not going to get it.' Her smile was cruel. 'The holiday's over. He's in deep enough. You're going to hit him this afternoon.'

'Orders?' He squinted his eyes against the brightness of the water. Velda shrugged. Cyril sighed and looked at his hands. 'We could be rushing things,' he said slowly. 'I don't think he's quite ready.'

'You're not paid to think.' Velda was curt. 'I know him better than you do — we're closer. I've worked on him. Play it right and there'll be no trouble. You might even manage to stay his friend. But it's got to be this afternoon.

'And you'd better fix those scales a little — just in case.'

★　★　★

Brad paused, his key hovering over the lock, assailed by a sudden giddiness. Not surprising really, fifteen hours hadn't been long enough to shake off the physical exhaustion of the previous night. He'd slept a little, eaten a little, had his hot shower but it hadn't been enough.

He blinked the burn from his eyes and stabbed the key at the lock. He missed. The door opened before he could try again.

'Brad!' Helen stood before him. Her eyes widened as they searched his face. 'Brad! Are you ill?'

'Just bushed.' He hadn't seen her since the previous day. He wondered what she would have said had she seen him in the early hours. It had been a long walk from where he had left Grenmae and he had practically crawled the last half mile. He hefted the books under his arm. 'Can I come in? These things are heavy.'

'Sorry.' She stepped aside. He entered, dropped the books on to a table, nodded at Serge.

'I had to borrow one of your suits,' he said to the captain. 'I didn't have a chance to ask — my own clothes were ruined.'

'That's all right.' Serge looked thoughtfully at the older man. Brad's face was grey, lined with fatigue, the face of a man who has done too much too soon. 'There was a report of a chasing last night,' he said. 'You?'

'Me.' Brad caught Helen's expression and quickly changed the subject. 'Hell, I'm tired. All this running about has knocked the stuffing out of me.' He sank in a chair. 'Where's Carl?'

'Gone.'

Brad raised his eyebrows.

'He's gone,' repeated Helen. 'He came here with a woman, Velda. He took his things and paid Serge what he owed him. Brad! I'm worried!'

'About Carl?'

'Yes. He's come into a lot of money somehow. He boasted that he had enough to live rich the rest of his life. And the woman, Brad. Velda. She was laughing all the time.'

'I didn't see her laugh,' said Serge. Helen frowned.

'She was laughing inside,' she insisted. 'As if the whole thing were a big joke. Almost as if she was gloating over something.'

'Maybe she was,' said Serge curtly. 'Maybe she was satisfied with a job well done.' He lifted his hand to cut short her protest. 'Now I've told you this before, Helen. Carl is his own boss. There's nothing you or I or anyone can do to stop his getting money by any means he sees fit. I tried to warn him about Velda but he wouldn't listen. I can't blame him. I had no right to interfere. If it hadn't been for you I wouldn't have bothered.'

'Serge is right, Helen.' Brad sensed the beginning of a quarrel and he didn't like it. 'Carl has a right to do as he wants.'

'To sell his body?'

'If he wants to — yes.'

'But — '

'Now listen to me.' Brad leaned forward, cursing the fatigue which dulled his thinking. 'In our own time people used to sell their blood and we thought nothing of it. This is merely an extension of the same thing. Carl has made his choice. He wants to live as rich and as high for as long as he can. His body is his security against his non-payment of debt. He knows this.'

'He was tricked,' said Helen bitterly. 'He was led into debt by that woman.'

Brad shrugged and looked at Serge. They both agreed on the same thing. It made no difference.

'He probably didn't even know what he was letting himself in for.' Helen fumed her anger. 'They could even have drugged him into signing the agreement.'

'No.' Serge shook his head. 'That's not possible. A man has to be declared sober, undrugged, unhypnotized and in his right mind before a notary will witness his deposition.'

'Then, if he hasn't yet signed?' Helen seized on the faint hope. Serge shrugged.

'He's been getting money from somewhere,' he pointed out. 'He must be heavily in debt. It may take a little longer, that's all, but the end result will be the same.'

'Unless the debts are paid?'

'Naturally — together with accumulated interest, but do you seriously think Carl could possibly pay off a heavy debt? From what I've seen of him he isn't the type to work most of his life on a subsistence level.'

'Would you?' said Brad. 'If you had the conviction that it didn't matter? That this life was a cage which you could leave at any time you wished — knowing that you would live again? All it requires is a little faith. Most of you seem to have it. Carl must have found it too.'

★   ★   ★

He leaned back in his chair wondering if he really believed what he had just said. Damn Grenmae and the twisting of his analogy. And yet the man had spoken sense and had reason for his belief. Carl must have acquired a similar belief. Or had been talked into accepting it. Was he being such a fool?

'Faith,' said the captain slowly. 'As a scientist, Brad, do you believe in such a thing?'

'It exists.'

'That isn't what I asked.'

'All right,' said Brad. 'Faith is the unquestioning acceptance of the existence of something without any proof that it exists at all. It is an emotional state leading to an emotional conviction which allows of no argument or rational discussion. It is basically a state of immature wish-fulfilment. It is an illusion bordering on insanity.'

'Now wait a minute, Brad,' said Helen. 'I have faith that the sun will rise tomorrow. Is that an illusion?'

'You have knowledge based on millions of years of repetition,' snapped Brad. 'That isn't faith. Faith, by its nature, cannot be proven or disproven. It is, and has to be, sufficient unto itself — or it isn't faith.'

He rubbed his forehead. The ache in his temples was getting worse, the muscles taut at the base of his skull, the minute quivering of his muscles a little more pronounced. He looked at the woman.

'Coffee, Helen?'

'Of course.'

She vanished into the kitchen and he relaxed, listening to the small sounds she made. He caught Serge's expression and felt a quick sympathy. A man needed a woman about the house. He felt a momentary regret that he had always been too busy to recognize the missing ingredient in his life.

'You were talking about faith,' said the captain. 'What has that to do with Carl?'

'Isn't it obvious? Reincarnation, in this world, is an apparent fact and — '

'Apparent!' Serge almost shouted the word. 'What do you mean?'

'Exactly what I say.' Brad remained calm. 'If you would rather not discuss it — ?'

'Carry on.' Serge looked up as Helen returned with the coffee. He took a cup, sipped, smiled his thanks. 'I'd like to know just what you're getting at.'

'I've studied the histories,' said Brad. He gestured to the pile of books he had collected from the library. 'Essential research if I'm to survive in this modern age. As a scientist I'm naturally sceptical and demand proof. Not faith but proof. You recognize the difference?'

'Naturally.'

'Good. Well, as far as I can determine, this whole thing started about twenty years after the Débâcle. Orthodox religion had been dying for years and the war just about finished it completely. The world had gone to hell and Mankind tottered on the brink of barbarism. Then, quite suddenly as these things go, reincarnation was an accepted fact.' He gulped his own coffee. 'How do you account for that?'

'Simple,' said the captain. 'Owing to the general shortage of anaesthetics the medical profession turned to the use of hypnotism as a form of anaesthesia. Naturally there were experiments. During the course of these experiments the principle of Breakthrough was discovered.'

'Correction.' Brad set down his cup. 'Hypnotic reversal techniques had been known long before the war but the findings of the investigators were unacceptable as proof at that time. Do you want me to continue?'

'Yes, but — ' Serge broke off as his voice rose in pitch. 'What you say means nothing. Many things have been learned more than once.'

'True, but does the intrinsic truth of a discovery alter according to when it is made?'

He had the captain trapped but it was a small victory. The conversation was too familiar. He had led others into verbal snares in the past but always they retained something he had never possessed.

Their faith, perhaps?

'You overlook one thing.' Serge rose and glanced at his watch. 'You assume that your own age was omnipotent. You thought that you knew all the answers but history shows how wrong you were.'

'We had proof.'

'Proof? Isn't that what scientists look for in order to confirm their own theories? Isn't proof selective to the experimenter? Maybe, Brad, your people made the wrong experiments.'

* * *

Brad sighed as he helped himself to more coffee. He didn't look up as Helen showed Serge to the door, the woman seeing her man off to work. They were in

146

love with each other, that was obvious, but he felt only a touch of envy. Jealousy was absent.

'Brad!' Helen sat opposite him, her face serious. 'Do you believe in reincarnation?'

'No.'

'Why not?'

'Because the thing is too pat. It strikes me as a gimmick designed to meet a pressing need. A tool developed to do a specific job. The fact that it was successful doesn't make it genuine.'

'You can't be serious!'

'I'm serious,' he said grimly. 'But listen and try and get this thing in its right perspective. We can make a pretty shrewd guess as to conditions after the Débâcle. A devastated country, industry smashed, little food, less education, a general, all-round mess. And then, suddenly, reincarnation. The one thing which could pick up the pieces and put them together again.'

She waited, not speaking, her eyes on his own.

'What else would have persuaded people to work for the future? Children?

Most of the things born about that time could hardly have been called that. Racial survival? Without a strong religion and the education we'd given our people before the balloon went up nobody would have cared a damn. Politicians? They'd destroyed us. The individual? He couldn't have cared less. We lived in a selfish world, Helen. It took a miracle to make people work like dogs without hope of immediate reward.'

'The miracle. Reincarnation?'

'It must be the answer. A deliberate, cold-blooded introduction of the one system which could save what was left of the world. It gave a personal stake in the future to every man, woman and child alive at that time. It gave the same thing to posterity. Someone in those days was a genius!'

'Or sincere,' pointed out Helen. 'You can't be sure, Brad. It could be perfectly genuine even if it came about as you say.'

'It could,' he admitted. The possibility had troubled him. 'But facts are against it. Why is there no one around who remembers our time? Why are they all from a long way back so that it's almost impossible to check their veracity. And why are there such things as cripples.'

'Serge is a cripple.'

'So?' Brad frowned, he had wondered about the captain. 'Did he try and explain it?'

'He said that cripples could, literally, be new-births. That they hadn't lived before and so couldn't remember the past.'

'Perhaps — it sounds logical.' He frowned then shook his head. 'But it doesn't make sense. New-births should only be possible if all the 'waiting list' of those who've lived and died are filled up. We know that the population of this world isn't anywhere near as large as our own. So — what's happened to the 'waiting list'?'

'I don't know.'

'And another point. There's another explanation for cripples. Maybe the reversal techniques don't work all the time. But they should. Why do they miss out at all?'

'Exactly. If the thing is a fake then why admit failures?' Helen rose and collected the coffee things. 'Why don't you get to bed, Brad. You look all in.'

He nodded and rose and went to his room. But he couldn't sleep. Going to the bathroom for a drink of water he halted by his drawing board. Something tucked down beside the chair caught his eye. It was small, only a trick of reflection had betrayed its presence. He picked it up and looked at it. He had never seen one before but he knew what it must be.

A bug.

An electronic ear.

Someone had listened in to every word.

10

Master Cartographer Lewis was a small man with liquid brown eyes, shoulder-length hair and a liking for floral perfume. His mannerisms belonged to the court of Charles II, but his clothing, dark maroon with the electronic symbol proud on his breast, was strictly modern.

'Ah, Stevens.' He waved Brad to a chair. 'Let me see now,' he mused. 'The last time we spoke was a week ago when you suggested that you might be of some use to this office.'

'That's right,' said Brad.

'And just what did you have in mind?'

'I think you remember that.' Brad eased his collar, wishing that the air-conditioning had been set to a cooler level. 'You agreed that I could be of service on the preparation of certain maps. I've worked on them since our conversation.' He lifted his folder and placed it on the desk. 'Here they are. I hope that you find them of some use.'

It was more a prayer than a hope. He forced himself to appear relaxed as Lewis leafed through the folder. The cartographer was impressed.

'Neat,' he mused. 'Very neat. Are you a draughtsman?'

'No. An atomic physicist.'

'Really?' Lewis blinked, then smiled. 'In the old days, naturally.' It was a condescending smile tinged with contempt. So might a modern physician have dismissed the claims of a witch doctor.

'Yes,' said Brad tightly. 'In the old days. Your people don't seem interested in my knowledge of the subject.'

'No? Well, they wouldn't, would they?' Lewis frowned at the maps. 'I'm afraid that these aren't of much use to us despite the careful workmanship. Our own maps are quite satisfactory as far as surface detail goes. I had hoped that you could have given us more specialized knowledge.'

'The location of valuable deposits?'

'Exactly. Such information would be of real value to the Guild.' Lewis rapped the tips of his manicured fingers on the little pile of maps. 'We are also interested in the Underground system of the city. As you realize much of the surface was destroyed during the Débâcle and still more is in an advanced state of decay. If the Underground route could be mapped with accuracy it would enable our engineers to by-pass some of the more dangerous areas. It is reasonable to assume that the radiation index of the lower levels would be lower than that on the surface. However — ' He broke off, staring at Brad. 'Are you ill?'

'No.' Brad dabbed at the sweat beading his forehead. 'It's just the heat. A temporary indisposition. It's nothing.'

'You look far from well.' Lewis registered genuine concern. 'A glass of water, perhaps?'

'No thank you.'

'As you wish, but you seem in pain. In such cases it is always wise to consult a lifeman.'

Inwardly Brad cursed the other's concern. If only this office wasn't so hot! He remembered to be polite.

'I'll be perfectly all right, but I'll

remember your advice. Now about the maps. I can't understand your difficulty. You will find a complete map of the Underground system in every station. You must have reached those on the outskirts by now?'

'We have,' admitted Lewis. 'But centuries of climatic change have not been kind to paper and paste. Also, from what remnants we have discovered, the maps appear to have been schematic diagrams rather than true portrayals. We cannot drill an opening from the surface without more accurate information. You know, of course,' he said casually, 'just where such maps are to be found?'

'Certainly. 55 Broadway, S.W.1.' Brad spoke without thinking then cursed himself for having given away saleable information.

'Is that Westminster?'

'Yes.'

'A pity. The entire area was demolished in the first hours of the Débâcle.'

'I see.' Brad felt a perverse satisfaction in learning that the politicians had not escaped. 'My information, then, is that much more valuable?'

Lewis acknowledged the statement with a slight bow. His fingers toyed with the maps.

'I must confess to a little disappointment,' he murmured. 'I had hoped — well, never mind. Perhaps you will be able to do better in the future?'

'Perhaps.' Brad rose and thrust the maps back into their folder. The heat of the office was making him sick. He had to get out into the fresh air and soon. 'I take it that you're not interested in these?'

'I did not say that.' The cartographer rested one slim hand on the folder. 'They are not as valuable as I could have wished but — ' His tone lost its affectation as he looked at Brad. 'You are unwell. Let me call the resident lifeman.'

'No.' Brad was curt. Medical attention would have to be paid for. And, though he did feel ill, it was due to natural causes. Lack of food and sleep — that was all. He forced himself to smile. 'Now, if we could come to some agreement as to the worth of these maps?'

The sum he finally received was, in

relation to the work he had done, about one third of what was paid to the lowest menial labourer.

★   ★   ★

He spent the lot on a meal.

He had steak and tomatoes and potatoes fried in butter. He had peas and a strange vegetable which once had probably been familiar but which had been mutated beyond recognition. He had a dessert of fresh fruit covered with cream and then sat with coffee and a pack of cigarettes and looked into his future.

He didn't like what he saw.

Since leaving the Cradle he'd proved himself to be a colossal failure as far as adapting himself to this new society was concerned. Barred from his profession he'd been like a chicken without a head. Morals, ethics, old-fashioned customs had clogged every step of his way.

He should have used Morgan, not turned him down flat.

He should have let that fool burn himself to death.

He should, at least, have taken Murrey's sword and jewels.

Instead he had spent too much time doing useless research, sponging on Serge while he pondered philosophical abstractions.

Savagely he ground out his cigarette.

'Something else, sir?'

The waitress was young, charming, eager to please. Brad wondered what kind of place he had chosen for his meal then realized he could be wrong. She was probably paid on commission or hoped for a fat tip.

'More coffee.'

He lit another cigarette while waiting, glowering at the white façade of the Guild Tower framed in the window. Damn Lewis and his meanness! Damn the snotty technicians who regarded him as little better than dirt. Damn them all to hell!

'Your coffee, sir.' The waitress showed him a generous expanse of shoulder and upper-breast, smiling as she set down the cup. 'If you want anything else — anything at all — you will ask, won't you?'

So, it was that kind of place. Brad gave a mental shrug as he picked up his coffee. He had no right to be critical. This was a new age with new customs and he was the odd man out.

He remembered the favourite statement of one of his professors.

'Survival is the test of intelligence,' the old man had been fond of saying. 'An intelligent man will be able to survive in the environment in which he finds himself. If he can't then he's proved that he's too dumb to live.'

A society was an environment and Brad liked to think that he was intelligent. Therefore he should have no trouble in surviving.

But — how?

Irritably he lit still another cigarette. He was smoking too much, eating too little, burning up his reserves and wearing his nerves to shreds. He was too old for this sort of challenge. He wished that he could be like Carl. He, at least, had solved his problem. Holden had come to grips with this society.

It was all a question of attitude.

Brad stared thoughtfully at his cigarette. He had made the statement and it was true. All he had to do was to accept the moral code of this time. And, for a man reared in the jungle of the twentieth century, that shouldn't be difficult.

'Something else, sir?'

The waitress was back with her toothpaste smile. Brad scowled, irritated at her for having broken his train of thought. Business must be terrible — he wasn't that handsome.

'No,' he said coldly. 'You've got nothing that I want.'

'Some wine, perhaps? We have a very good selection. Or spirits? Gin, rum, brandy, scotch — '

'Scotch.' Brad smiled. The waitress smiled back.

She had what he wanted.

★   ★   ★

The docks lay on the curve of the estuary, sheltered from the open sea by a long mole tipped with the squat tower of a warning beacon. Brad stared at the cluster of vessels, small craft mostly with a scatter of luggers and trawlers. Sailing boats for the most part with a couple of square-rigged clippers moored in deeper water. He spotted the occasional funnel of a steamboat, the smooth lines of a rare diesel and something which could only have been a hydrofoil. All were armed.

It looked like a marine museum.

He joined a cluster of men bunched on the wharf watching some activity in the harbour. Small boats filled with men formed a rough circle. The water between threshed with hidden violence.

'They've got it,' said a man in a thick, blue jersey. 'Stuck it good. It shouldn't take long now.'

'A dozen harpoons,' sneered a weather-beaten oldster. He spat in the water. 'In my day we'd have taken care of a thing like that with a couple of boathooks and a knife.'

The first man grunted, ignoring the boast, shielding his eyes against the sun. He swore as something like a whip rose above the water and smashed at one of the boats.

'The fools! Don't they know better than to get within reach? Another couple of yards and they'd have been stove and sinking.'

'What goes on?' Brad touched the man on the arm. He answered without turning.

'Kraken. It must have got swept in with the tide. Probably dying but the more savage because of that. It's lucky it was spotted before it could tear up the farm.' He grunted with satisfaction. 'It's all right now. They've got it.'

Brad swallowed as he saw what the men had caught. The body was as big as a horse, the frill of viciously clawed tentacles at least twenty feet long. A dozen lines held it fast.

'Are there many of those?'

'Not in the shallows. They stick to deep water most of the time where the big fish are. But they're cunning. Sometimes they'll follow a ship for days hoping to snatch a man. But there's not much danger as long as you use nets.' He looked curiously at Brad. 'Do you want to ship out?'

'No. I'm looking for something. A ship from Scotland. You know her?'

'The *Laird of Stirling*? Down at number fifteen.' He jerked a thumb. 'Just keep going and mind your head.'

The warning was genuine. The wharf was littered with ropes, cluttered with gantries and heaps of discharged cargo. A small train puffed furiously as it dragged loads to the warehouses. Men shouted as they handled boxes, bales and barrels. Twice Brad had to duck as loaded slings swept above. The smell of fish and salt was overpowering.

The *Laird of Stirling* was a tubby, broad-beamed sloop with patched sails, scarred timbers and a wreath of net. The hatches were closed. A gangplank ran from the side to the wharf. A man leaned on the rail and glared at Brad.

'Is this ship from Scotland?'

'Aye. What d'ye want?' He was coarse, surly, rudely abrupt. His kilt was stained with salt and grease. His face raw from exposure. 'We've no place on this ship for ony Sassenach, ye ken.'

'I want to see Jamie Macdonald,' said

Brad. If this character was an example of the type of men the Highlander hoped he would work with then he was an optimist. Not that it mattered. Brad hadn't come to accept the offer — he was merely putting theory into practice.

'Who?'

'Jamie Macdonald. He's expecting me.'

The man startled Brad with his sudden hoot of laughter. 'Why ye richt — '

'Enough!' The word held the lash of command. An elegant figure, lace at throat and wrist, looked down from the bridge. 'Show the stranger to my cabin, Jock. And mind — ware your tongue and treat him with kindness.'

'Aye,' snarled the man. 'As my captain commands.' He scowled at Brad. 'Will my laird be pleased to follow me the noo?'

The cabin was small, laced with heavy wooden beams, lined with racks of weapons. Large-bore shotguns for the most part, an effective defence against the creatures of the deep. A lantern swung in polished gimbals above a table littered with papers. The captain swept them into a drawer and produced a bottle and glasses.

'You'll be taking a dram,' he said and poured before Brad could accept. He passed over a generous measure of whisky. 'Your health!'

The scotch was good, stronger than Brad had known and with a smokey, peat flavour which teased his throat and tongue. He felt it warm his stomach as the captain refilled his glass.

'Your health!'

Again the captain refilled Brad's glass and he wondered if the man hoped to get him drunk. The thought made him cautious. There was something odd about the man. He was elegant enough, more so than Jamie, but his face was older, stamped with a hint of slyness, a trace of malicious humour. His eyes sparkled with it as he looked at his guest.

'You were asking for Jamie,' he said. 'He expects you?'

'Yes. Is he here?'

'No.' The captain sipped his whisky, dabbed at his lips with a scrap of lace. His manners and accent were those of a cultured man. 'Our Jamie's had to go ashore. You know how it is with ships.

Cargoes to sell, others to buy, all the detail of provisioning and trade. Of course I know what goes on, Master — ?'

'Stevens,' said Brad. 'Brad Stevens.'

'Ah!' The captain carefully lowered his glass. 'The sleeper?'

'That's right. You've heard of me?'

'I have indeed.'

'From Jamie?'

'Who else?'

Brad smiled. This was going to be easier than he'd hoped. The captain was obviously in a position of authority and would have access to cash. All Brad had to do was to persuade him to pass some over — and then make sure they never met again. The beauty of it was that, in this society, he would be committing no crime. It was not the duty of the police to protect fools.

'Then you know all about it,' said Brad. 'Good. What I came to see Jamie about was a matter of expenses. There are certain debts I must settle before I can leave.'

'For the north?'

'That's right.' Brad was feeling good,

the scotch was taking effect. 'And I shall need some equipment. It's specialized stuff and I'd better get it here to make sure of it. I guess a couple of thousand imperials will take care of it. You'd better let me have the money now. We don't want to waste any time.'

It was, he thought, a neat way of putting it. He wondered why the captain was smiling.

'So you intend going with Jamie Macdonald to the north and giving him the benefit of your skill. Is that it?'

'Yes.' Brad felt uneasy.

'You know little of the Highlands?'

'Not much. Why?'

'I thought not.' The captain moved to stand before the single door. 'If you knew more you'd have known that I wasn't wearing the tartan of the Macdonalds. I am a Campbell. You've made a sad error, Master Stevens.'

11

The bunk was too short, tight to his shoulders, cramping to his hips. Brad winced as he tried to ease the ache in his legs. They had tied the bonds too tight and his hands were numb. The lump on his head was giving him hell.

Bitterly he stared into the darkness. He could have been unconscious for hours or for minutes, he had no sure way of telling. But no light penetrated the seams of the deck or hull and, somehow, it felt as if it were night. He moved his head and winced again. He'd been a fool to try and fight his way from the cabin — an even bigger fool to have got into this mess in the first place. But how could he have known?

Two ships, of course, that part was obvious. Two clans, obviously at intense rivalry, and he had picked the wrong one. An even chance of being right and he'd lost. His luck was running true to form.

He wondered just how genuine Macdonald had been.

In this world you couldn't tell. When a man could remember a previous life as if it had been yesterday old wrongs and hates took a long time to die. He probably remembered Glencoe when, in 1692, a chieftain and thirty-seven Macdonalds had been massacred at the hand of the Campbells. It could be that he hoped for revenge. The captain had entertained no doubts.

'He'll be wanting you to make weapons so as to avenge Glencoe. I know our Jamie. It's been a sore point with him for many a long year. He has ambition for his clan and hates us Campbells. Well, maybe he has cause for that. But if I let you fall into his hands there'll be black war in the Highlands. That I cannot allow.'

It was then that he had tried to fight his way from the cabin.

The ship rocked. The wet slap of waves sounded against the hull at his side. The bow dipped, rose, dipped again. Brad tensed to a new fear. They were sailing and taking him with them to the north

— if they didn't throw him over the side on the way.

It wouldn't be murder. The sea would kill him — not they.

Savagely he tore at his bonds. The ropes were firm but the bunk was not. His extra height gave him good leverage and he thrust with his legs and felt something give a little. Desperately he threshed against the sides and wood cracked, snapping with the brittle sound of age. He thudded to the deck and tore his hand on the sharp point of a nail. After what seemed an age he brushed the shredded rope from his wrists.

'Are ye awake doon there?' A flood of light poured down the companionway as a man peered into the lazarette. A messenger sent by the captain to make sure that he was still alive. Brad's groan needed no art to make it sound realistic.

'Are ye not well?' The man stepped forward, blocking the light of the deck-lantern, squinting down the short flight of steps. He could see nothing but shadows. Brad reached out, picked up a heavy fragment of the bunk, groaned again.

It was too much for the man. He clattered down the few steps and stooped over the shattered bunk. Before he could rise Brad slammed the club against the base of his skull.

He hadn't killed the man. He wasn't even sure that he'd knocked him out but he didn't stay to make sure. Quickly he climbed the steps to the deck. It was night. Far to one side the light of the beacon threw itself over the water. Farther back, like a cluster of distant stars, lights shone from the dock-area. They were just outside the mouth of the estuary.

'Hold!' A voice roared from the bridge. 'You there! Hold that man. Don't let the Sassenach escape!'

Brad grabbed the deck-lantern. The hot glass scorched his fingers as he poised it for the throw. It arched towards a pile of deck-cargo, a sheet of flame springing over the lashed bales. It gave him time. Men, rushing to seize him, automatically turned to quench the flames. In the confusion Brad leapt for the rail.

He had forgotten the nets. They

wreathed the deck in close-meshed protection. He hit them, bounced back, sprang to his feet as the captain barked fresh orders. Frantically he swarmed up the mesh, hung for a moment on the sagging support, then flung himself into the sea.

Half-way to the water he remembered what the nets were for.

★ ★ ★

It was very quiet. The stars blazed down from a midnight sky, familiar constellations, so close that it seemed as if he could reach up and touch them. Brad didn't try. If he did he would sink and it was taking all his strength to keep afloat. He had long since given up the struggle against the tide. All he could do now was to lie on his back and trust to his natural buoyancy.

He wondered how far he was from shore.

The ship had long since vanished. It had circled him once and had thrown out a mess of garbage. Something had eaten the garbage. Whatever it was had apparently been satisfied. Brad hoped that it would continue to stay that way.

A wave slapped his face and he coughed, remembering not to struggle. As long as he breathed and made no constrictive movement he would continue to float. He might look like a log or resemble a corpse but he was alive. And, eventually, the tide had to turn.

Another wave slapped his face. Something touched the top of his head. Something wet and clammy trailed along the back of his hand. He grunted, threshed — and sank two feet into mud.

A freak current had driven him to shore.

He climbed to his feet and waded through an endless expanse of rush-covered mud. The Dengie Marsh probably, he was certainly north of Shoeburyness. He wondered what had happened to Southend.

Then he hit solid ground and fell flat on his face.

He woke to sunshine, a soft breeze, the mournful honking of geese. Something stabbed sharply into a shoulder. He turned and saw the sharpened end of a pole. A bearded face stared down at him from the other end of the crude spear.

'You don't look a hunter,' he said.

'I'm not.' Brad rubbed the dried salt from his eyes and sat upright. He looked a mess. He'd kicked off his shoes and clothing while in the water and was naked but for shorts. Dried mud blackened his feet. A long weal on one thigh oozed blood. He wondered what had caused it.

'Jellyfish,' said the stranger. 'What happened?'

'I jumped a boat.' Brad doubled to a sudden fire in his stomach. 'They were taking me north and I didn't want to go.' He felt vomit rise in his throat. 'Have you got any water?'

He retched before the man could return. The water was thick with sediment, carried in a rusty can. Brad gulped it and was immediately sick again.

'You ill?' The stranger remained well out of reach. Brad drank more water and sat, sweating.

'I had a big meal yesterday,' he explained. 'The food must have been too rich. Then I had a lot of exertion and — '

He doubled again as his stomach rejected the water. He remained bent over, fighting the pain in his belly, feeling the touch of a terrible fear.

He had known such pain before — no! It had to be the food.

'Look,' said the stranger. 'If you're a runner there's nothing for you here. There's too many of us as it is. Foraging is bad and I'm scared that hunters might spot us. Maybe you'd better try farther down the coast. You can have the water but that's all.'

'I'm not a runner.' Brad climbed cautiously to his feet. The pain had died and with it the fear. He managed to grin as he staggered and almost fell. He was exhausted but that was to be expected. 'I told you, I was kidnapped. Damn it, man, you've got no cause to be afraid of me.'

'Maybe not.' The stranger was thoughtful. 'Kidnapped, uh? Are you a lifeman?'

'A doctor.' It was no time to be honest. 'I've got some medical knowledge. Why?'

'We've got a man who's pretty sick.' The stranger hesitated, then stuck out his hand. 'My name's Weston.'

'Stevens,' said Brad. 'Brad Stevens. Where is this man?'

He was lying in a rough shelter made of woven branches buried deep among the trees which had encroached almost to the edge of the marsh. A small fire smouldered to one side of the bed of fern. A woman squatted beside it bathing the face of the sick man with a damp rag. Weston touched her shoulder and jerked his head. Rising she left the hut.

'He's been like it for days,' said Weston. 'He seems to be getting worse. Do you know what's wrong?'

'Don't you?'

'You're the lifeman. You tell me.'

'All right.' Brad had learned the textbook symptoms of radiation poisoning only too well. He looked at the sores on the hands and mouth, touched the febrile skin. 'He's dying. He's been somewhere hot and collected a massive dose. There's nothing I can do to help him.'

'I warned him,' said Weston helplessly. 'I told him not to take chances but he wouldn't listen. Are you sure there's no hope?'

'Not unless you can give him continual blood-rinse and have the chemicals and drugs to combat the cellular decay.' Brad turned from the sick man. 'The Institute could maybe save him. Why don't you take him there?'

Weston grunted his contempt.

'All right,' snapped Brad. 'So it was a stupid suggestion. Now tell me why.'

'He's a runner.'

'So what? Do they have to know?'

'They'd know.' Weston led the way from the shelter. The woman stared hopefully at them. The hope died as he shook his head. 'I'm sorry, Mary,' he said gently. 'There's nothing we can do.'

She swallowed and went back to her nursing. Weston looked suspiciously at Brad.

'You're not a hunter,' he said. 'You're not a runner and you're certainly not a lifeman. Don't you know that whenever you need medical attention or enter into a

176

contract for debt they give you a quiz? They hypnotize you and you have to tell the truth. You can't avoid it.' He shifted his grip on the spear. 'Now,' he said dangerously. 'Just who the hell are you?'

Brad told him. Weston blinked, shook his head, then shrugged.

'I wouldn't know,' he said. 'I've been on the run for three years now and I'm out of touch. But I'll tell you this, friend. If you're a spotter for the hunters I'll give you cause to regret it.'

'You'd kill me?'

'I wouldn't have to. This thing through your guts would take care of it. So I'd owe your medical bills, so what? It'd just be more money that I haven't got.'

He meant it. Brad looked at the rough spear and shuddered. He could imagine the damage it would do. Then he trod on a stone and winced.

'I need shoes,' he said. 'And clothes. Can you fix me up?'

'Maybe.' Weston returned to the hut. He came out bearing clothes. 'He won't need them any more,' he explained. 'You might as well use them if they fit.' He saw

Brad's expression. 'It's all there is,' he said. 'You can figure out some way to pay his woman later. Now, do you want them or not?'

*   *   *

The shoes were too big, the clothes too small. Brad eased his shoulders as he sat watching the central fire. It burned under a blackened pot which contained something which smelt like stew. What was in it he didn't care to guess. Hedgehogs, perhaps, snakes, even rats, anything which would sustain life. The community couldn't afford to be particular.

He looked around as he waited for one of the women to dish out the meal. Like the hut in which a man lay dying other shelters rested among the trees. The place looked something like a gipsy encampment but there were no horses or caravans. Not even any kind of wheeled vehicle. When these people moved they carried all they owned.

He guessed there must be about a score of men and a half-dozen women. He had seen no children and doubted if there were any. These people, all debtors on the run, wouldn't want to add to their troubles. But that was something they didn't have to worry about. Lurking at the edges of the poisoned areas, entering into them from ignorance as often as not, would quickly have made them all sterile.

It must be a hell of a life.

He wondered just how many other groups there were like the one he saw.

'I don't know.' Weston spooned stew from a bowl and smacked his lips over a bone. It was a small bone with a familiar shape. There would be frogs in the marsh. 'Quite a few, I guess. I know for a fact there's another farther to the north and there used to be a scatter of loners to the south. Hunters got them.' He drained his bowl. 'Aren't you hungry?'

'No.' Brad handed him his share of the stew. 'Is that why you band together? Fear of the hunters?'

'Not exactly. It tells against us in a way. Too many people leave too many traces and makes us easy to spot. But what sort of a life is it alone?'

Brad could imagine. He stared thoughtfully at the fire as Weston finished his meal. Man was a gregarious animal and was unhappy unless he had company of his own kind. But why should they have run in the first place?

They owed money, yes, but the pay-off wasn't too terrible. Not in this world where the worst that could happen was the loss of a few years of life. And what was that to a man who was convinced that he would live again?

He turned to ask the question and felt Weston tense at his side.

'What — '

'Shut up!' The man cocked his head as if listening. Deep in the woods something whistled, a bird Brad thought.

'I was going to ask — '

'Hold your tongue!' The bird whistled again, closer, then a third time, closer still. Weston cursed and sprang to his feet. The spear looked like a stick in his hand. 'Hunters! Damn you! You led them to us!'

'No!' Brad jerked to his feet, sprang aside from the threatening point. 'I had nothing to do with it!'

'Jack!' A man came bursting from the wood. He was gasping, his eyes wild. 'To the south and west,' he panted. 'A big body of them. We've got to make a run for it!'

'Warn the others!' Weston gestured towards the huts. 'No noise. Leave everything we can do without. Move off to the north in pairs. Scatter and make for Finnegan's Point. Make certain you aren't followed.'

'Right!' The man hurried away and the camp boiled in a sudden confusion. There was no panic and little sound, only a frantic desperation. Mary came running from the sick man's hut.

'Jack! We can't leave Harry. You — '

'We've no choice,' snapped Weston grimly. 'They're on us, Mary. Get your things and move out with Joe. Hurry now!'

'But — '

'Damn you, girl! Hurry!' He swore as a woman tried to pick up the cauldron and burned her fingers. 'Leave it, you fool! Run!'

Brad stepped back to the shelter of a

tree. He didn't know what was going on but he wanted to get out of it. He didn't move fast enough.

'You!' Weston spotted the movement. 'All right,' he said. He was sweating, moisture trickling into his beard. 'I warned you what would happen if you led them to us. Well, damn you, here it comes!'

He laid the point of the spear against Brad's stomach.

And pressed.

12

There was a sound like a giant cough. Weston jerked, his mouth opening in shocked surprise, his eyes suddenly vacant. Then he fell, collapsing at the knees, his body as limp as wet tissue paper. A tuft of feathers stood out from one shoulder. The spear rasped an ugly scratch across Brad's stomach.

'Hold it!' yelled a voice. 'Freeze, all of you. We've got you surrounded!'

Brad sagged against the tree as men poured from the woods. His mouth was dry at his narrow escape and he had an almost overwhelming desire to run. He forced himself to stay where he was. The man who had shot Weston could just as easily have gunned him down and he wanted to offer no temptation. He looked up as someone called his name.

'Brad!'

Carl came towards him. He was dressed in camouflaged overalls, steel helmet and campaign webbing. He cradled a thick-barrelled gun in his arms. He looked remarkably cheerful.

'Well, well,' he grinned. 'As they say, it's a small world. What the devil are you doing here?'

Brad told him, cutting it short, looking curiously at the activity around. Other men, dressed as Holden, were crowding the bunch of runners into a compact knot in the centre of the clearing. One of them kicked out the fire.

'Nice catch,' he called to Carl. 'You sure knew what you were doing. The biggest bunch I've seen for a long time. Nice work, Carl.'

'Training,' said Carl. He smiled at Brad. 'I used to be in the Territorial Army back in the old days. There's nothing like a touch of military discipline on an operation like this. Get into position. Let them spot you on three sides and grab them as they run to the other. Simple.'

Brad shook his head. He was still bewildered. He looked down at Weston. 'Is he dead?'

'No, just knocked out.' Carl hefted his

weapon. 'This thing fires hypodermic needles. If we leave him alone he'll wake in a couple of hours, stiff as a board and with a king-sized headache. Why was he trying to stick you with that pole?'

'He thought I was working with you.' Brad felt sickness rise in his throat at the thought of what might have been. Carl stared at him, leaned his gun against the tree, produced a flask.

'Here. Take some of this.'

The brandy burned his throat but warmed his stomach. Brad smiled as he handed back the flask.

'Thanks. Do you mind telling me what all this is about?'

'Later.' Carl looked up at the sun and then at his men. 'We've got to get this lot on their way.' He raised his voice. 'All right, chain 'em up and start back at the double. Use your whips if you have to but make good time.' He relaxed as the file of men and women vanished among the trees. 'You'd better travel with me, Brad. I've got a truck and there's no sense in walking when you can ride.'

'How about the others?'

'The boys know what to do. There's a boat waiting to pick them up lower down the coast and they can handle things from now on.' He picked up his gun, turned, stumbled against Weston. 'Damn it! I'd forgotten him.'

'There's a sick man in one of the huts,' said Brad. Carl raised his eyebrows.

'Bad?'

'Dying.'

'Then he can die in peace.' Carl grunted as he stooped and hobbled Weston's feet and lashed his hands. He plucked out the missile and tucked it into a bandolier. From a pouch he took a hypodermic and injected its contents into the man's arm. After a few moments Weston stirred and opened his eyes.

'Up!' snapped Carl. 'You're too big to carry. Up on your feet and start walking.'

'Can't you leave him?' said Brad. 'Let him go?'

'No.' Carl was emphatic. 'And before you get all soft and sentimental, Brad, remember that this character tried to spill your intestines.' He kicked Weston in the side. 'Come on now! Get up!'

'Damn you!' Weston strained at his bonds as he climbed painfully to his feet. He glared at Brad. 'I was a fool to have trusted you. I should have left you on the beach. You damn hunters are probably feeling proud of yourselves. Well, I'll know better the next time.'

'Hunters?' Brad was beginning to understand. He looked questioningly at Carl. 'Is that what you are?'

'Hell, no,' said the young man. 'I'm a debt collector.'

★   ★   ★

'It's decent work,' said Carl. 'More fun than scavenging and it takes less time.' He spun the wheel and sent the light truck jolting past a twisted mass of gnarled roots. Brad grunted as he bounced on the hard seat. Weston, lying inert in the back, made no sound.

They had been travelling for an hour and Carl was talkative. His success had loosened his tongue and he wanted to boast. He had, he felt, something to boast about.

'The expenses are high, of course,' he continued. 'The boys work on a contingent basis but I have to provide the equipment. Even so the profits can be high. A runner usually owes a mint before he takes off and I get a percentage of all debts owing. This bunch should really bring in the loot.'

'Why do they do it?' asked Brad. 'Run, I mean. What do they hope to gain?'

'How do I know? I guess they're just plain scared and want to hang on to what they've got.' Carl shifted gear and sent the vehicle snarling down an avenue of stunted growths. 'Not long now before we reach the river.' He settled back and lit a cigarette. He passed the pack to Brad who helped himself. He carefully broke the match before throwing it over the side. Carl sneered at the action.

'Frightened of fire? This stuff's too damp to burn.'

Brad shrugged.

'So you're the cautious type,' said Carl. 'That's the trouble with you, Brad, you're too damn cautious. Me, now, I'm willing to take a chance. That's why I'm rolling home to collect and you're just a passenger. Give it time and you'll be like that character in the back. Living like an animal because you owe more money than you can pay.'

'If that happens then you can hunt me down,' snapped Brad. Carl shrugged.

'That's their word for it. As far as I'm concerned it's just a matter of collecting debts. I can't worry about the feelings of a lot of stupid cripples.'

'Cripples? Like you?'

Carl smiled. He didn't answer. Brad felt a sudden suspicion.

'Carl! Have you — ?'

'That's my business!'

'But — '

'As I said, Brad, you're too cautious.' The woods thinned as they jolted over a wide expanse of uneven ground. Ahead lay the shimmer of water. 'I'll bet that you and Helen imagine I'm all kinds of a fool. Right?'

'You trust that woman too much,' said Brad. 'And that playboy you run around with.'

'Cyril?' Carl shrugged. 'I used him.

And Velda's all right. You've got to take people as you find them, Brad. They helped me.'

'Got you in debt, you mean.'

'So what? Back in the old days most people lived in debt all their lives. I would have been one of them. So what's the odds? This world isn't all that different to the one we knew. Unless you manage to get a stake you stay on the bottom. Well, I've got my stake. Now I'm putting it to work. This collecting business, a share in a couple of cargoes, some antiques. I'm thinking of opening an electrical store, service and repair, and I've other ideas. Do you know they don't have dog racing in this world? Or speedway? Or bingo? I tell you, Brad, a smart man can make his way anywhere. I'm smart.'

'Maybe others are smarter.' Brad dragged on his cigarette, a little jealous of the other's achievements. 'Cyril for one. You think that you used him — I think that he cheated you. He could still be cheating you. How could you be sure?'

'I'd know.' Carl's voice thickened as his

big hands clamped on the wheel. 'If that character ever tried anything like that — '
He shook his head, then resumed his grin. 'You're a pessimist, Brad. You're too old for this kind of life.'

'Too old to carry the amount of debt you've managed to accumulate,' snapped Brad. 'How the hell do you hope to pay?'

'I'm paying. As long as I keep ahead of the interest they can't foreclose.'

'And if you can't?'

'I can. I will.' Carl reached down and dragged on the brake. The truck halted at the foot of a small pier. A boat waited at the end. 'About Velda, Brad. I'm going to marry her.'

Brad tensed but managed to hold his tongue.

'You're smart,' breathed Carl. 'Had you made a crack about her I'd have broken your jaw.'

'It's your business,' said Brad stiffly. 'I wish you luck.'

'Thanks.' Carl dropped from the truck and led the way to the boat. A man sat beside the outboard motor. He rose and saluted as Carl approached. 'Class,' said

Carl. 'You've got to put on a front. The way to show these people that you've got money is to waste it like hell. Once they think you're rich they'll back you all the way.' He stuck out his hand. 'So long, Brad. See you around.'

'At the wedding?'

'Maybe.' Carl released his grip and nodded towards the boatman. 'He'll take you to the city and drop you off somewhere where you can find a cab. You got money?'

'No.'

'You have now.' Carl passed over a bill. 'And, Brad, take some advice?'

'Such as?'

'Get a grip of yourself — and stop being a cripple!'

★   ★   ★

He was dead.

The heart had stopped, the lungs, the rushing pulse of blood and air. Ten billion tiny suns flickered into darkness as the cells died into inert protoplasm and, like the dying glow of a filament, his consciousness dissolved into eternal night.

Death came to greet him.

Death was tall, thin, skeletoid. Dark pits swarming with shadows rested to either side of the gaping hole of the nose. But Death was amused. Death wore a smile.

'Hello, Brad,' he said. 'Did you really hope to escape?'

It seemed as if he protested.

'A few hundred years — what is time to me?' Death shrugged with the dry grate of bone. 'I can afford to wait, Brad. I can always afford to wait. You all come to me in the end.'

There was the sound of liquid bubbling. Death wavered and, suddenly, wore a familiar face.

'A bad business, Stevens,' said Sir William. 'Absolute rest and quiet could, perhaps, prolong life for a short while but the end result is inevitable. The time element is, unfortunately, small.'

Sir William vanished and Jack Murrey took his place. His mouth was wreathed in the rictus of his dying snarl so that, he too, seemed to be amused.

'Damn yer eyes, ye stinking poltroon! I'm waiting for ye in hell!'

Then he fell while all around him came the clanking of tankards on the wooden boards, a metallic sound which went on and on and . . .

Brad jerked awake, drenched with perspiration, heart hammering against his ribs. Blankly he stared at the familiar walls of the apartment, the drawing board, the chair in which he had fallen asleep. But the dream persisted. He could still hear the metallic sound. The doorbell sounded. Staggering to his feet he opened the panel. Velda, eyes snapping, stared into his face.

'About time,' she began then; 'Hey, you on a jag or something?'

'What do you want?' He clutched the edge of the door for support. 'Carl isn't here.'

'I know. I want to talk to you.' She stepped past him into the apartment. Too weak to argue, Brad slammed the door. He recognized the danger signals from his stomach and headed for the bathroom. He reached it just in time.

He retched, his stomach heaving and seeming to be filled with hot embers. He ran water from the tap, drank, retched again. A phial in the cabinet contained pain-ease tablets and he swallowed a handful. Stripping he stood under the shower and let the ice-cold spray numb his febrile skin. The tablets were strong, they jerked his pain-level to the ceiling and, when he stepped from the shower, his agony had dwindled to a dull ache.

Grimly he stared at himself in the mirror.

He looked ghastly. His skin was grey, his eyes bloodshot, his mouth a thin, bloodless line. Carefully he shaved, brushed his teeth until his gums bled, slicked back his hair. The clothes Weston had given him were filthy and stank of death. He kicked them aside and, naked, padded into Serge's bedroom where he helped himself to fresh clothing.

'Nice.' Velda nodded as he returned to the living-room. 'You've a decent body, Brad.'

He had forgotten the woman.

'You look better,' she said critically.

'Not much, but a little. What's wrong? Need a fix?'

'If I want dope I'll buy it.' He searched his pockets. 'Have you a cigarette?'

She lit two and passed him one, watching him through a veil of smoke. There was a poise and assurance about her every gesture and he could understand how Carl had succumbed.

'I hear that you're getting married,' he said. 'May I offer my congratulations?'

'For what?' Her eyes were very cool. 'It won't be the first time and I doubt if it will be the last.'

'Does Carl know that?'

'I'm not worried what Carl thinks. He's a nice boy but marriage isn't forever.'

'Like death?'

'That's right.' She smiled up into his face. 'But you don't believe that, do you, Brad? To you death is a one-time event. You're born, you live, you die — finish! A hell of a philosophy!'

'We managed to live with it for a long time,' he said. 'But how do you know what I believe?'

Her smile was enigmatic.

'I found a bug in here,' he said slowly. 'Someone planted it so as to listen in to what we were saying. You planted it. Why?' He frowned at her silence. 'All right — then who wanted to listen?'

'Wrong question.' She blew a smoke ring, watched it coil across the room to break on his chest. 'Try again.'

'What do you want?'

'That's better.' Deliberately she stared at him and, for a moment, Brad had the impression that he was naked again. There was nothing amorous about her scrutiny. It was more as if she were the potential backer of a fighter and wanted to gauge form. He could have been a horse. He remembered that he had seen her stare at Helen in exactly the same manner.

'You know,' she said abruptly. 'I like you.'

'Why?'

'Does it matter? Maybe we've more in common than you think.'

'Age perhaps?'

'Perhaps.' She ignored the biting sarcasm. 'Age — or experience. But we can talk about that later.' She rose, opened her handbag, took out a card. 'Marc Veldon wants to see you.'

'So?' He ignored the pasteboard, feeling sweat begin to bead his forehead, the action of the tablets beginning to fade. 'Should I be flattered?'

'Veldon's rich. He can afford to buy what he wants and pay well for what he gets.' She pressed the card into his hand. Automatically he took it. 'Don't be stupid, Brad. Go and see him.'

'And if I don't?'

'Then,' she said deliberately, 'I might have cause to feel sorry for you. Very sorry.' She turned and walked towards the door, hesitating with her hand on the knob. 'Tomorrow, Brad,' she said. 'Early.'

She didn't wait for his answer.

Alone he hurried into his bedroom and found what he was looking for. Grimly he read every word and checked each item. At the end he knew what was wrong with him.

He wasn't ill — he was dying.

He had known this pain before and, slumping into a chair, the bill from the

Life Institute in his hand, he knew that there had been truth in the nightmare. Death was waiting and Death could afford to smile.

He hadn't been cured.

Three hundred and thirty-eight years in the Cradle and he was back in square one. Back where he'd started. Dying of cancer!

13

'Interesting.' Edward Maine pursed his lips as he riffled through the sheaf of fluoroscopes, x-rays and pathological reports. It was an act, he had studied them in private, but Maine was something of a showman. 'You know, Stevens, I've never seen anything quite like this before.'

Brad grunted from where he sat in a chair glowering over a cigarette at the Master of Hypnotic Therapy.

'There seems to have been a sudden and extremely violent explosion of rogue tissue from at least three dormant foci. The stomach, spleen and lower bowel are in a dreadful condition. The pain must have been intense.'

'It was.' Brad drew at his cigarette, filled his lungs with smoke, exhaled. He felt a little light-headed from morphine, a little weak from three days in bed during which time he had suffered exhaustive testing. 'What's the verdict?'

'The prognosis? Death, naturally.'

'When?'

'Very soon.' Maine sounded encouraging. 'The system will not long be able to withstand the invasion of such masses of cancerous tissue. There will be a physical breakdown, of course, but I don't think that it will last for any appreciable time. The pain, naturally, will be accumulative in its intensity.'

'Yes,' said Brad tightly. He remembered the pain. He doubted if he could stand more of it. 'What do you suggest?'

'Euthanasia.' Maine was definite. 'There seems little point in waiting unless, that is, you wish to undergo the experience to its full. I cannot recommend it. The danger with painful and violent death, self-induced death, is that though the danger is always potential, the Death Trauma is so intensified that Breakthrough sometimes becomes impossible.' He sighed. 'It is something I wish these loopers would understand. The danger of crippling yourself is hardly worth a new experience.'

'I'm no looper.' Brad leaned forward, crushed out his cigarette, met the lifeman's eyes. 'When I was resurrected I understood that I was completely whole and cured. You discharged me on that understanding. I agreed to your charges on that belief. Now you tell me that I'm dying of the same complaint I suffered when I first entered the Cradle. It seems to me that someone isn't playing fair.'

'I don't understand.' Maine was stiff. Brad snarled.

'I figure that I've been cheated. By you. By the Institute. Is that plain enough?'

The room became very quiet. Only the slight noise made by the attendant novice as he adjusted his weight broke the stillness. Brad caught the sound but didn't look at the young man. Maine was in no danger of physical attack — he didn't need a bodyguard, but Brad wondered how often a patient went berserk. Often enough, that was obvious, or there would have been no need for the watchful attendant. Then Maine sighed.

'You wouldn't know,' he said quietly. 'I

must excuse your insult on the grounds of ignorance. You cannot know what you are saying.'

Brad recognized his anger and realized that he had gone too far. He had, in essence, spat in the face of the King. Or accused a nun of being a harlot. But he still had to be satisfied.

'I'm sorry.' He looked down at his hands, not trusting his eyes. 'I did not mean to offend. But you can appreciate the shock. I thought I was cured. When I left here I was convinced of it. And now — '

'I understand.' Maine could afford to be gracious. 'I accept your apology.'

'Then,' said Brad tightly, 'perhaps you will be good enough to explain?'

'The explanation is simple. When you left here you displayed no sign of cancer. I did mention that the present outbreak must be from previously dormant foci. In that case, of course, they would not have been recognizable.'

'Dormant!' Brad stared his disbelief. 'When I entered the Cradle,' he said distinctly, 'I had advanced cancer of the stomach and lower bowel. It was inoperable — that's why they put me away, to await a time when such things could be cured. And now you sit there and tell me that you spotted no signs of such a condition? Did you look?'

'We looked.'

'Are you sure? Helen and Carl, the other two, they had suffered from over-exposure to radiation. Time would cure them. Did you automatically assume that I suffered from the same complaint?'

★   ★   ★

He had been shouting. He realized it as the novice rose and stepped towards him, realized too that he must seem like a man about to lose his temper, perhaps to go berserk. To kill and die killing under the compulsive need for emotional release.

'All right,' said Maine quietly. He wasn't talking to Brad. 'Resume your seat.'

The novice hesitated, then obeyed. Maine didn't look at him, his eyes held Brad's.

'We have here,' he said in the same quiet tone, 'a problem. Two sets of opposed facts. Let us assume that both are true. You displayed unmistakable signs of advanced cancer when you entered the Cradle. I found no such signs. Something, then, must have happened to produce that effect. It is remotely possible that your body managed to repair itself — such things can happen during long periods of complete rest and quiet. But cancer is not a disease in the true sense of the word. It is a violent and uncontrolled growth of normal cells which are harmful, not beneficial to the body. It is not an organic disease or a malfunction of bodily chemistry. You understand?'

Brad nodded.

'Let us progress. What was said to you as you entered the Cradle?'

'Uh?'

'What was said to you? What were the last words you heard?'

'I — ' Brad frowned, trying to remember. 'I think it was something like 'You've nothing to worry about',' he said. 'Something like 'You'll soon be better'.'

'Are you certain?' Maine was very intense. 'Please be precise.'

'I think — no!' Brad remembered the smiling face touched with concern. Doctor Lynne trying to be cheerful. What had he said? 'I remember now,' said Brad. 'It was 'When you wake your troubles will be over'.'

'Are you positive?'

'Yes.'

'I see.' Maine relaxed. He was smiling. 'When you wake your troubles will be over,' he mused. 'You were under sedation, of course. Your body completely relaxed. Your mind tranquil. In a perfect condition for a hypnotic command. Your subconscious accepted the words as such and, when you woke, your troubles were over. You no longer displayed signs of cancer. It is possible that the original outbreak had dissipated in some way, the rogue cells assimilated into the body, unwanted tissue which the subcellular blueprint of the body had disposed of. You know, Stevens, this is all very interesting. Given a long enough period and strong enough hypnosis, who can tell what might be accomplished?'

'Not me.' Brad couldn't share the other's enthusiasm. 'And I don't really care. All I know is that I'm dying of cancer.'

'True.' Maine returned his attention to his patient. 'Perhaps the original foci retained their life or other foci could have been stimulated into activity. The point is academic.' He slipped the sheaf of reports back into their folder. 'Well, I'm glad that we've managed to clear that up, Stevens. Did you want to see me about anything else?'

'Wait,' snapped Brad. 'I still want to live. What could be done? How about regrafts?'

'Body-replacements?' Maine nodded. 'It is always possible but I must be frank. In your case there would be complications.'

'Money?'

'That isn't my department,' said Maine stiffly. 'I was talking from the viewpoint of operative procedure. Your original cancer was caused by exposure to radiation which, in a sense, seeded you with cancerous foci. Now, in order for a regraft to be effective the natural resistance of the body to what is, in a biological sense, a foreign body must be overcome. This is done by extensive irradiation. You see the danger?'

'I see it.' Brad fumbled for a cigarette, lit it, found comfort in the familiar smoke. 'The irradiation could easily set up new foci so that I'd be back where I started.'

'Exactly. And there is another factor to be taken into consideration. The world isn't as you knew it, Stevens. The race has changed. The years following the Débâcle did much to eliminate certain traits and weaknesses. Diabetes, haemophilia, epilepsy are unknown now. Only the strong could survive. There was a period of ruthless culling and the establishment of affinitive types. And there was a lot of radiation with consequent mutation. In short — it may not be easy to find suitable regrafts for your body.'

'But they could be found? It isn't hopeless?'

'No,' Maine admitted. 'But it may take

time — and it will be expensive.'

'Yes, I suppose so.' Brad tasted blood and realized that he had bitten his lip. 'But, damn it, there's a chance!'

It was all that mattered.

★ ★ ★

The Life Institute was fronted by a broad flight of steps sweeping up to the huge, ever-open doors. They made fine seats if you didn't mind the hardness and the curious glances of the passers-by. Brad cared for neither. Locked in his own world he sat and stared into the distance and, though the sun was warm, he couldn't rid himself of an inner chill.

He was going to die.

He had always been going to die but now it was different. Now he had to count life in days instead of years, hours even. He couldn't be sure. He could only be certain of one thing. Without morphine he was going to suffer the agony of the damned — and he had no morphine.

The accountant had been adamant.

'I'm sorry but, really, your debt is

already far too large for us to be able to extend further credit. After all, we are carrying you to the further extent of your examination and consultation.'

'That's generous of you.'

'Amazingly so.' The accountant had missed the sarcasm. 'It is only because Master Maine feels a certain sense of responsibility toward you that agreement was reached, but that is as far as we can go.'

'Am I supposed to drag out what's left of my life in agony?'

'Of course not, we aren't savages. Euthanasia is free in such cases as yours. Your debt, in that case, well — 'The man had tried a little humour, ' — we can't win all the time, can we? Every organization has some bad debts — yours will be one of them. Now I don't suppose you want to wait too long. Shall we make an appointment for euthanasia now?'

Brad hadn't made the appointment. He hadn't managed to gain credit for morphine either. Money could buy it at any drug store but he didn't have money. Money could do so many things. It could even buy him the chance of continued life.

He glowered and lit another cigarette.

The worst part was how they had all managed to make him feel as if he was stupid and a little peculiar. The receptionist, the attendants in the wards, Maine, the accountant, even his fellow patients once the word had got around. He was dying and, instead of pity, they had only displayed a controlled impatience. He was dying — so what?

Where was the problem?

It was a natural enough reaction — for them. He would have felt the same towards a medieval man in need of an appendectomy. What was there to worry about? Just have the operation and get it over. It's just a sleep and a wakening. But, to such a man, an operation of that nature would be tantamount to death. He simply wouldn't have been able to believe that he would wake again. It was just a question of viewpoint.

Brad was still a medieval man.

The cigarette burned his fingers and he threw away the butt, watching it fall, the thin column of smoke rising from the damp cylinder, wavering as it neared extinction. Automatically he reached into his pocket for another cigarette. His fingers touched pasteboard and he drew it out and looked at it.

It was the card Velda had given him. Marc Veldon's card.

Veldon — who was rich.

14

The room was an inverted bowl of tinted glass, the air tanged with the scent of pine, the carpet so deep and rich that it was like walking on a cloud. Baroque statuary lined the walls interspersed with fragments of decaying art. Small tables bore other pieces of craftsmen's skill; a set of chessmen carved from amber, a scattering of Victorian paperweights, a figurine of hammered brass.

Brad wandered among them, finally pausing to pick up a piece of jade, running his fingers over the cunningly shaped surface, a little surprised at the tactile pleasure it gave.

'A beautiful piece,' said a voice behind him. 'It is an endless pity that it represents a lost art.'

Marc Veldon smiled at Brad as he turned. He was of medium height, stooped and thin. His face was creased, his mouth a gash, his eyes peered from beneath bushy

213

brows. A mane of white hair fell down to his collar. He looked a worn sixty-five but was probably older.

'Ninety-eight,' he said, and lifted a hand. 'No, I am not a telepath, but I have lived long enough to learn how to read expression. Your curiosity was apparent.'

'Satisfy it some more. Why did you want to see me?'

'Perhaps I too am curious. It isn't often that I have the opportunity of talking with a man older than myself. Does that answer your question?'

'No,' snapped Brad. 'I would suggest that you had some other reason.'

'Of course.' Veldon shrugged. 'That must be obvious. But I forget myself. Would you like some refreshment? Tea, coffee, alcohol — morphine?'

'No, thank you.' Brad felt himself tense. How much did this man know?

'As you wish.' A glint appeared in the deep-set eyes. 'I hope that you are not going to prove a difficult man, Stevens. I expected you long before this.'

'I came when I was ready,' said Brad evenly. 'You probably know why I was delayed.'

'I know. But I am not accustomed to be kept waiting — not even when other matters seem to have a higher priority. It would be as well for you to remember that.'

Veldon, Brad thought grimly, was typical of his class. Then he remembered his own desperate need and swallowed his pride.

'I apologize,' he said. 'I didn't realize the matter was urgent.'

He had said the right thing. Veldon, mollified, gestured to a chair.

'Let us talk.' He waited until they were seated. 'As you guessed I did not send for you to assuage idle curiosity. As it happens I have seen all three of you sleepers before and know one quite well.' He made a peculiar hissing as if laughing inwardly at some secret joke. 'Very well indeed.'

'You are talking of Carl Holden?'

'Who else? He is strong, healthy, a little wilful and very much of a fool, but that is the fault of his brain not of his body. How long would you say he has to live?'

'What?' Brad was startled by the

question. 'I'm not certain. About fifty years. The life expectancy of my time was close to eighty.'

'Eighty years,' said Veldon softly. 'How fortunate you were — and how foolish to throw away so much. You know, Stevens, when I was born I could look forward to, with luck, no more than fifty years of life.'

'The Débâcle?'

'Yes. The poisons spread then are only slowly dying and cellular disintegration caused by radiation has a direct bearing on age. People now do not live as long as they did.'

'But,' said Brad dryly, 'there are exceptions. You, for example.'

'I am a ghoul. Most of my body originally belonged to other men but there is a point beyond which regrafts are no longer possible.' Veldon paused. 'I have reached that point.'

'Then you will die?'

'No!'

He was defiant and, as he rose and paced the floor, Brad realized that, to Veldon, the prospect of death was intolerable. The man read his expression.

'You wonder why I should fear death,' he said quietly. 'I am not a cripple. I know that I have lived before and will live again. *But as what?*' His gesture took in the room, the furnishings, his whole, personal empire. 'Will I be as rich? As powerful?'

'Does it matter?' Brad couldn't understand the man's mania. Surely life was more important than money. 'You could always rebuild.'

'Do you think I would be given the chance? I — ' Veldon broke off, sweat gleaming on his face and Brad guessed that he had been about to say too much.

And, suddenly, he realized that Veldon was not only very rich but very much afraid.

★   ★   ★

They left the chamber roofed with glass and entered another lined with luminescent panels. The pine of the air gave way to a raw, animal-like odour. A monkey squatted in a cage. Veldon leaned against it, blocking the animal from view.

'We spoke of death,' he said. 'Ordinary,

217

physical death, but why should men have to die at all? That is a question I have been trying to answer for thirty years.'

'Have you found the answer?'

'I have. It is merely an extension of regrafting techniques. If a man can give me his stomach to replace my own then what is to stop him giving me his entire body? That is the problem I set my lifemen and technicians. How to success-fully transplant a human brain from one body to another. The results are in this cage.'

Veldon stepped to one side and gestured towards the interior. The monkey squat-ted in one corner aimlessly plucking at its fur. A thin cicatrice ran around its shaven skull.

'Look at it,' urged Veldon. 'Tell me what you think.'

'It seems to be in fine condition,' said Brad cautiously. He wondered what the man was trying to prove. He scratched at the bars of the cage and the animal turned to look at the sound. The eyes were wild and without focus. 'How are the reflexes?'

'Slow.'

'Motor co-ordination?'

'Perfect. Don't judge wholly by what you see. The animal has been kept under sedation but the tests are conclusive. The operation has been perfectly successful.'

'How many?'

'Operations?' Veldon shrugged. 'I can't really say. We had many failures, naturally, but this is the tenth consecutive success. This particular operation is now merely a matter of routine.'

'I see.' Slowly Brad straightened and looked at the older man. 'And now, I suppose, you carry it on to its logical development. You try it on a higher order of life.'

'On men,' said Veldon. 'Naturally.'

'Men!' Brad drew a deep breath. 'Where can you find such volunteers?'

'I don't. There is no need. I buy what is required.'

'Of course,' said Brad. He thought of Weston and knew now why the man had run.

★ ★ ★

'You seem disturbed,' said Veldon. 'Some coffee?'

They had returned to the chamber roofed with glass where refreshments stood on a table and the air was heavy with culture and good taste.

'Thank you.' Brad accepted the cup. 'Do you intend escaping physical death by having your brain transplanted into another man's body?'

'Of course.'

'Holden's?'

'So you guessed.' Veldon smiled as he helped himself to more coffee. 'Delancy is an associate of mine and was perfectly willing to sell me Holden's debt. At a profit, naturally. More coffee?'

'Not at the moment.'

'You are calm,' said Veldon. 'I like that. I had half-expected some foolish emotional outburst but Velda was correct in her estimate of you. You did well to come to me, Stevens.'

'Perhaps. Does it have to be Holden?'

'Yes. His nucleic acids match mine to a favourable degree and there are other advantageous factors which cannot be denied.'

'His potential longevity?'

'That, too, is important,' agreed Veldon. He sniffed at his coffee. 'I'll be frank, Stevens. Holden is the best subject I could hope to find. I do not intend losing him.'

'You may have no choice.' Brad felt an overwhelming desire to shatter the man's arrogant confidence in his plans. 'Carl has ideas of his own. You may not be able to foreclose on his debts.'

'You are talking of his enterprises,' smiled Veldon. 'They are doomed to failure. I control the companies and speculations in which he is interested. A year, two years, I can give him that. I shall not be ready before then.' His smile grew wider. 'Of course, you could attempt to warn him, but I think you will be wasting your time. Holden is an optimist.'

And he would have a wife who would keep him rigidly in line. Brad could see where Velda fitted into the pattern. He wondered about himself.

'Tell me, Stevens,' said Veldon abruptly. 'Do you believe in reincarnation?'

'You know the answer to that,' said Brad

tiredly. 'You know I found the bug you had planted in my chair. The answer is no.'

'So I understand. I find it hard to believe.'

'I don't give a damn what you believe,' snapped Brad. He was tired of pandering to this ghoul. 'I think that a man has only one life as we know it. What happens after death is something I shall discover one day but I can't imagine that I'll return with a full set of memories.'

'I know of your views on the subject. I'm glad that you have not changed them.'

'Why? What's it to you?'

'In this world you are unique. You are in the happy position of not having to worry about the future. No one else, not even the cripples, can be certain that they will not be reborn. That gives you a unique power. I can use it.'

'How?' Brad frowned, wondering what the man was getting at. Slowly Veldon finished his coffee and set down the cup.

'I am a rich man,' he said evenly. 'I have enemies. It would be most convenient for me if I could have those enemies — eliminated.'

'Murdered?'

'If you prefer the word, yes.'

'And you expect me to become your tame assassin?' Brad wondered if Veldon were sane. 'You honestly think that I would consent to murder?'

'Why not? You are an intelligent man.' Veldon smiled from the depths of his chair. 'Intelligent enough to realize that you must have money to enjoy yourself.' He leaned forward a little. 'And what is it to you? You have no feelings for my enemies, no regard. It isn't as if you were really killing, not in the sense that you use the word. You would be merely accelerating a natural process. I wonder that you hesitate to accept.'

Brad almost told him, then remembered why he was here. He still needed money. And he was curious.

'This unique power you talk about,' he said dryly. 'Just what is it that I'm supposed to have?'

'You have no fear of the future,' snapped Veldon promptly. 'You have no dread that you will ever be called to account for anything you may have done in this life. Death, for you, is the end. That is why I can use you.'

Brad nodded. Things were beginning to make sense.

'I will pay you well,' said Veldon. 'I need a man I can trust and you could be that man. You will live in luxury with a special bonus for — every occasion.' His voice became even more persuasive. 'I am sure that you are in need of money.'

He was more than sure, he was positive, but Brad guessed that he didn't know the whole story. Not that it mattered.

'I've heard words,' he said flatly. 'As yet I've not seen any of this money you keep talking about.'

'You would like proof?' Veldon rose and opened a cabinet. He turned holding a sheaf of bills. He peeled off some and tossed them on the table in front of Brad. 'Two hundred imperials as a token of good faith.'

Brad ignored them.

'If you're looking for a bargain,' he said flatly, 'you've come to the wrong shop. Five hundred and we start talking the same language.'

'Very well.' More bills fluttered to the table. This time Brad didn't hesitate. He rose as he tucked them into a pocket. 'Is that all?'

'For the moment, yes. I shall contact you.' Veldon waited until he had almost reached the door. 'One moment, Stevens.'

'What is it?' Now that he had the money Brad was in a hurry to get out and go shopping. 'What do you want?'

'I want you to remember something. You know how I intend to obtain the raw material for my transplanting experiments. Well, I have arranged to take over the debts of both yourself and of your friend Helen. Need I say more?'

'No,' said Brad thickly. 'I understand.'

The ghoul had him trapped.

15

The model paused, turned with calculated grace, swayed back along the catwalk to the veiling curtains beyond. A scatter of applause rose from the audience. A scented fop, resplendent in silk and lace, a convoluted wig on his head, jewelled shoes on his feet, minced forward with congratulations.

'*C'est magnifique!*' he lisped. '*Vous êtes une —* '

'I'm sorry,' said Helen. 'I don't speak French.'

'*Incroyable!*' The fop waved a lace-draped hand, his shrug a perfect example of the arrogance which had once led him to the guillotine. 'Your designs are superb,' he said painfully in English. 'Sheeman is fortunate to have found you. The Marquis de Chatillon will tell him so.'

'Thank you.' Helen tried not to laugh as the fop minced away then turned to receive other congratulations. They were effusive but those from the buyers were the important ones.

'You look happy.' Serge stood behind her, very tall and masculine in the scented softness of the salon. 'I take it that the collection was a success?'

'Serge!' Helen reached out and took his hands. 'I didn't expect you. Did you see the parade?'

'I've only just arrived.' A fat matron cannoned into him, throwing him against Helen, giggling a quick apology. 'Well, was it?'

'A success? I think so. Sheeman seems happy and the buyers are interested.' Helen smiled her pleasure. 'I haven't felt so good since I woke. It's nice to have found a place in the world, to be able to stand on my own feet.'

'Is it?'

'Of course! I couldn't let you keep me for ever.'

'No,' he said flatly. 'I suppose not. Well, I just looked in to see how things were going. I'll see you around.'

'Serge!' She caught his arm as he

turned away. 'Is something wrong?'

'No. Why should there be?'

'That's what I'm going to find out.' She led him to an alcove, an oasis of quiet in the general noise of the salon. 'All right,' she said firmly. 'We're both adult people so let's stop acting like children. When are we going to get married?'

He blinked his surprise.

'Don't you want to marry me?'

'Of course!' His hands were tight on her upper arms. 'You know damn well I'm in love with you and have been since we met but — '

'But now that I'm successful you don't want to take advantage of the past — is that it?'

He nodded.

'And before, when I had nothing, you didn't want me to feel indebted to you.' Helen shook her head. 'I suspected as much. I didn't think that I could be that unattractive. You fool, Serge! Why do you have to be so much a gentleman?'

'I'm not,' he said bitterly. 'I want you and you know it. But there's something you've forgotten. I'm a cripple.'

He was serious and she didn't make the mistake of passing it off as a joke. To the handicapped their affliction is never a joke.

'You idiot,' she said softly. 'You wonderful idiot. Have you forgotten that I'm a cripple too?'

★   ★   ★

The waiter bowed, proffered the bottle for inspection, drew the cork with a flourish and poured a little of the wine for tasting. Carl sipped it, pursed his lips, looked his disgust.

'What is this stuff?'

'Wine, sir. What you ordered. Is something wrong?'

'It tastes like red ink. Take it away and bring me something fit to drink.' Carl glared as the man hesitated. 'Well? Do you want to argue about it?'

'No, sir.' The waiter bowed, removed the bottle and soiled glass, headed to the back regions. He was scowling as he passed the guard. The cellarman reflected the scowl as he hefted the opened bottle.

'Red ink, eh?' He snorted his disgust. 'One of the best names in the business. A top vintage year and he says it tastes like ink.' He lifted the bottle, sipped, smacked his appreciation. 'Nothing wrong with this.'

'Do you want to go out there and tell him that?' The waiter jerked his head towards the restaurant. 'He's a big guy and the fellow with him isn't much smaller. I'd say they're both a little drunk. Give me something else to keep him quiet.'

'Wait a minute.' The cellarman grabbed an empty bottle, transferred the contents of the rejected one, added a spoonful of some mixture and gave it a shake. Deftly he rammed home a cork. 'Here. I've sweetened it and darkened the colour. See if the louse likes it this time.'

Going to the door he watched as the waiter carried over the bottle. The guard, wise in the ways of catering, smiled and spoke from the corner of his mouth.

'What odds he doesn't take it?'

'One'll get you five if he bounces it.' The cellarman grunted as Carl nodded to the waiter. 'An easy imperial. You can do

230

it all the time.' He frowned at Carl's companion. 'Do I know him?'

'Cyril Uwins. A leech.' The guard delved in his pocket, handed over a note. 'I've had my eye on those two. If they start anything I'm ready.'

'You think they might?'

'I've warned 'em once already. This is no place to have a quarrel.' He remembered something. 'Like to give me a chance to get even?'

'Sure.'

'Same odds that they don't blow up soon. That bottle should do it.' He sucked in his breath at the sound of raised voices. 'Quick! Is it a bet?'

'You're on!' The cellarman swore as a bell rang behind him. 'Let 'em wait. This I've got to see.' He chuckled as Carl rose to his feet. 'Looks as if you've lost again, Joe. The party's — God!'

Carl had risen. Cyril looked up at him and said something. He was laughing. He stopped laughing as Carl snatched up the bottle and smashed in his skull.

'Joe!' screamed the cellarman. 'He's killed him!'

Joe wasn't listening. Gun out he wove between the tables yelling for the killer to freeze. Carl snarled at him, flung the smeared bottle at his face, dived towards the exit.

'Block all doors!' The guard, blood streaming from a broken nose, lifted his gun and fired. The flat, ugly report stilled the sudden clamour. Carl skidded to a halt as a second guard blocked the door. He turned, ran towards the kitchens, changed direction as Joe blasted a shot at his legs. Desperately he headed towards the windows, the balcony outside.

A narrow ledge ran below the balcony. Carl swung his leg over the parapet, dropped to the ledge, began to inch his way along. Ahead were other windows, a chance to escape the guards, to gain time in which to think and plan. He didn't make it. His foot slipped and the wind tore between him and the building. An invisible hand pressed against his chest. The invisible talons of gravity clawed him out and down to the street below.

He screamed once before he hit the ground.

Holden wasn't dead. He lay, stripped and supine, a pale, corpse-like figure beneath the transparent lid of his capsule. His head was encased in plastic bandage. Thin pipes ran from beneath the covering to couplings in his container. The soft whirr of pumps gently vibrated the air.

'What happened?' Brad kept his voice low from instinct. Serge moved uncomfortably at his side.

'He and Uwins had a quarrel. People sitting close heard it and they say it was about a woman. Carl was warning Uwins to stay clear. He was about to leave when Uwins made a crack. Carl went berserk, killed him, tried to run for it. He didn't make it.'

'End of report,' said Brad dryly. 'What happens now?'

'I tie up the loose ends.' Serge hesitated. 'Look, Brad, there's nothing you can do. Why don't you just go home?'

'I'm staying.'

'But — ' Serge broke off as a lifeman entered and approached. He was a round,

233

fat, jolly man. He rubbed his hands to warm them against the chill of the compartment and smiled at the captain. Serge showed his identification.

'Captain Westdale, temporal police. Holden is guilty of murder. Please report as to his physical state.'

'Murder!' The lifeman looked grave. 'A terrible thing, Captain. I'd heard something about it, of course, but the matter was so urgent that — '

'Your report, please.'

'Uh? Oh, of course. Well, the brain is severely damaged. The skull received most of the force of impact. The cranium was shattered and splinters of bone driven into the cortex. If you would prefer the medical terms?'

'Thank you, no. What of the body?'

'Superficial damage only. The left collarbone, upper left arm and three fingers of the left hand are broken. Two ribs and the pelvis are cracked. There are various abrasions but nothing serious. A short spell in the amniotic tank and he should be as good as new. Aside from his brain, naturally.'

'Are you certain that his brain is damaged beyond repair?' Brad wondered why the captain was so insistent. 'Will you sign a deposition to that effect?'

'Certainly. As a governing mechanism the cortex is a useless mass of crushed and damaged tissue. We have introduced electronic devices to stimulate the motor functions of the body together with an artificial blood supply. His body will live, Captain, but, mentally, he is already dead.'

'Then why don't you bury him?' snapped Brad. He shivered, more from the atmosphere than the chill. The place reminded him of a morgue. The lifeman was shocked.

'Dispose of him? My dear sir, we simply can't do that. The Institute is quite satisfied as to the property rights of the body and full arrangements have been made with the owner. You see, all we have to do is to heal the damage, a relatively simple matter, and then keep him in stasis until his owner requires delivery. There is no problem aside from expense. You understand — er?'

'Stevens. Brad Stevens.'

'Ah, the name is familiar, I am acquainted with your case.' The lifeman beamed his pleasure. 'You should be interested in this new technique. In fact you are responsible for our perfecting the system. We learned much from your resurrection. Stasis has tremendous potential and should prove a wonderful success. There are always scavengers who have been careless and suffer from over-exposure to radiation. A term of stasis can effect an easy cure. Then, too, there are those who for various reasons would like to spend twenty, fifty or even a hundred years in healing sleep. Stasis can provide such a service.'

'Yes,' said Serge shortly. 'This is all very interesting, lifeman, but may we get back to the business at hand?'

'Certainly, Captain. I am aware of the procedure. I will send you the signed and witnessed deposition. However, I can assure you now that Holden will never, in this life, pay for his crime.'

It was, thought Brad, an odd way of putting it.

Outside he hesitated in the cool corridor, a question teasing at his mind. If stasis had been developed from experience gained during his resurrection shouldn't there be money in it for him and Helen?

Serge quashed the hope.

'As I remember it,' he said slowly, 'we argued that point to an agreement. Crow wanted to charge you for time, trouble and research necessitated by experiments conducted on your behalf. We opposed on the grounds that you were not in a position to give consent to the expense — and won.' He gave a short laugh of admiration. 'Trust Crow, the crafty devil! Now I understand why he didn't argue about it. No, Brad, I'm sorry. The Institute doesn't owe you a thing.'

'It was just a thought.' Brad felt his shoulders sag a little. A polished door threw back the reflection of an ageing, haggard man. Deliberately he straightened.

'Odd, meeting you here,' said Serge as they walked down the corridor. 'How did you learn about Holden?'

'By accident. I called here on another matter.' Brad had been shopping for morphine. 'I heard people talking and went to find out what I could.' He remembered the still figure in the transparent case. 'The poor devil!'

'Save your pity.' Serge was harsh. 'He committed murder.'

'He killed a leech,' said Brad coldly. 'In my book that makes him a destroyer of vermin.'

'He still took a man's life,' said Serge impatiently. His shoes echoed from the polished floor with a series of dull, flat sounds. 'Damn it, Brad, you can't defend his actions like that! Surely, in your time, you had laws against murder too?'

'Yes, but we took circumstances into consideration. Murder had to be a deliberate act with intent to kill. What Carl did wasn't murder as we recognized it. He lost his temper and struck out at a tormentor. That's manslaughter.'

'Not to us.' Serge halted, his face serious. 'If you kill a man who attacks you or tries to rob you, that isn't murder. If you kill a man in fair fight, a duel for example, the same. Killing a man to stop him killing others is permissible, but that's about all. Killing in temper, for profit, for kicks, because you turn looper or go berserk makes no difference. You've killed and that's the end of it. You've got to pay.'

He turned and continued striding down the corridor. Brad followed him, eyes clouded with thought. He had touched on something, the captain's reaction had been unexpectedly violent. And there was something else he couldn't understand.

Take a society in which death was nothing but a temporary sleep. A world which had stemmed from anarchy and in which the law was apparently weak. In such a civilization violence should be an accepted part of living with murder and assassination commonplace affairs. For, if everything else had changed, one thing would remain.

Human nature would be what it had always been. Men were still motivated by hate and greed and naked, primeval violence lurking always beneath the veneer of culture.

And yet, men did not murder.

They went to their death in strange and horrifying ways and submitted to the demands of their creditors but they fought the inclination to kill. For some reason they were afraid of the brand of Cain.

Brad asked Serge why.

'That was an odd thing to ask.' The captain halted and stood very stiff. Brad remembered that, as a policeman, he could not be expected to take the subject lightly.

'I want to know, Serge.'

'Why? Are you thinking of killing someone?'

'Perhaps.' As a joke it fell flat. Serge saw nothing humorous in the answer.

'Murder is the vilest crime there is,' he said shortly. 'You should know that.'

'All right,' said Brad tightly. 'I belong to a generation which tried to murder the world. You don't have to remind me. You don't have to preach either. I asked a question. I'd like an answer — not a sermon.'

'I'm not giving you one!' Serge made an effort to control himself. Brad had touched him on the raw. 'And I wasn't thinking of your past. Murder is vile because of what is done to the killer. Like Holden, for example.'

'What about him?' Brad was puzzled. 'Carl can't be hurt now. He's beyond your reach. You can't punish him.'

'Wrong,' said Serge grimly. 'We can. We will.'

'Now you're being ridiculous.'

'No, Brad, never think that. Do you know how we punish a murderer? We make him a zombie. Do you know what that is?' He didn't wait for an answer. 'They're animals, Brad. Beasts of burden — and it doesn't end there. We take their brains and encase them in metal. We attach devices to them so that they are fed with artificial blood and kept alive and conscious. Then we attach other devices and put them to work.'

'The living dead,' murmured Brad. Serge nodded.

'You've heard of them, everyone has. They are cheaper than any computer.

They have no mobility, no free choice. If they are stubborn they are punished — an electrode buried in the cortex stimulates the pain centre. They have nothing to do but work and wait for organic death.'

Wait! With their memories!

16

A thin chime echoed through the air. A soft voice, beautifully modulated, followed the fairy-bell echoes.

'Captain Westdale. Calling Captain Westdale. Come in, please. Captain Westdale — '

'I'm wanted.' Serge left Brad, crossed to a communicator, pressed the button. 'Westdale here.'

'Room 532, Captain. Official.'

'I'm on my way.' Serge broke the connection and returned to where Brad was waiting. 'Coincidence,' he said. 'Sometimes it happens and, when it does, it can be put to use. This has to do with what we were talking about. You'd better come with me.'

'A case?' Brad was curious.

Serge gave a non-committal grunt. 'It could be. Now stay close and on no account must you interfere.'

They walked to the far wing of the

243

building, took an elevator to an upper floor, walked down a corridor to room 532.

Within, on a bed, lay a boy.

He was about eight years of age, slightly built, a lock of blond hair hanging over his forehead. His eyes were closed. A hypnotic device hung from the ceiling above the cot and a trolley bearing an assortment of instruments and drugs stood to one side. Three adults occupied the room. One came forward as they entered.

'I am Master Hypnotist Lacey,' he said. He nodded to the other man. 'Novice Lifeman Saunders.' His head tilted to the woman sitting quietly watchful in a chair. 'Recorder Norden, Resident Notary.'

'Captain Westdale, temporal police,' Serge flashed his identification then gestured towards Brad. 'Brad Stevens, Observer.'

'The sleeper?'

'That's right. Here for educational purposes.' Serge looked at the sealed recorder, the check-camera. 'Everything seems to be in order. Shall we proceed?'

'By all means.' Lacey looked towards the cot. 'The subject achieved Breakthrough a short while ago and, during routine quiz, revealed evidence of the previous crime of murder. We immediately halted investigation and notified your office.' He smiled at the captain. 'I must say that you were very prompt.'

'I was in the building,' said Serge shortly. At times like this he had no desire for small-talk. He looked at the woman. 'Well, let's get on with it.'

The notary threw a switch. The recorder and camera came to life. Then the preamble; time, date, persons present, reason for recording. Then the waking, a simple matter of command. The boy opened his eyes. They were blue. He stretched and smiled a little. Then came the questions.

'You were born James Allen Pertwen,' said Lacey. 'You are aware of this?'

'Yes.' The voice was high, a childish treble.

'Your previous name was Frank Yendal. You are aware of this?'

The boy swallowed. Was it only

suspicion or did his eyes hold fear? Brad wondered but remained silent as Lacey repeated the question.

'You are aware of this?'

'No. I don't know what you're talking about!'

The boy was lying. It was written on his face but an expression wasn't enough. Lacey glanced at Serge and together they moved from the cot to where Brad was standing.

'A natural defence reaction,' said Lacey. The boy couldn't hear him but the recorder could. 'I'm certain that he is lying.'

'Perhaps he isn't,' suggested Serge. 'He could be telling the truth as he knows it.'

'A protective barrier?' The hypnotist shook his head. 'That is always possible, of course, but not, I feel, in this case. Breakthrough was complete. It is a question of simple lying. However, deep hypnosis can arrive at the truth.'

'I would prefer a waking admission,' said Serge. 'It is always far more conclusive.'

'Suggestion, then,' decided Lacey, and

led the way back to the cot. 'Frank Yendal!' he snapped. 'Pay attention!'

'But I'm not — '

'You are James Allen Pertwen but, before entering this life, you lived as Frank Yendal. You remember this?'

'Well — ' The boy was reluctant. His voice seemed a little deeper. 'No. That is I can't — '

'All right,' said Lacey gently. 'I'll help you to remember.'

★   ★   ★

He touched a switch and the hypnotic device sprang to life. Trapped by the swirl of colour the boy's eyes tried to escape, found it impossible, grew a little glazed. Lacey signalled to the novice.

'Light trance,' he ordered. 'Concentrate on the diminishing of fear.' He joined Serge where he stood beside Brad. 'A bad one,' he commented. 'I don't want to shock him more than I have to but the trauma is very strong. His sense of guilt is bolstering a natural apprehension. We must break down his reluctance to

247

admit what happened.'

'Murder!' Brad noticed that Serge was sweating. Lacey looked grave.

'It looks like it, Captain. There must be a strong reason for this defensive lying. But he won't be able to hold out for long.' He returned to his patient. Brad looked on with interest.

'Is this standard practice?'

'Yes.' Serge took out a handkerchief, dabbed at face and neck. 'Everyone is entitled to free routine processing at the age of eight. If Breakthrough isn't achieved then a second attempt is made at ten — a third at twelve. The quiz is a part of the standard procedure.'

Brad nodded, his eyes thoughtful. *Murder will out!* claimed the old adage, but he would never have guessed how the pious hope had turned into cold reality. He touched Serge's arm.

'If he confesses,' he whispered. 'Are you going to arrest him?'

'Yes.' The captain's face was drawn. 'That's the part of this job I don't like. I know better but they still seem like kids. Physically they are kids and yet — '

He swallowed. 'Shut up, now! Lacey's getting somewhere!'

The hypnotist's voice was a soothing drone.

'All right now,' he said. 'You remember that whcn you came here we sent you back — right back — until you remembered that once you were a man named Frank Yendal. You remember all this?'

'Yes.'

'Good.' Lacey reached out, turned off the hypnotic device. 'Now, you are fully awake and aware. You are oriented in space and time. You are James Allen Pertwen, born eight years ago. You are aware of this?'

'Sure.'

'Good. You were also Frank Yendal. You remember this?'

'I — Yes. Yes, I remember.'

'That's better. Now you have no reason for fear. It is perfectly natural that you should remember this man. You are one and the same. You understand this?'

'Of course.'

'Conditioning!' Brad gripped Serge's

arm. 'Damn it, the man's a hypnotist! The boy will believe anything he's told!'

'No!' Serge's answering whisper was emphatic. 'The boy is fully awake and aware. There is no possibility of the planting of false memories. The recorder and camera see to that — the entire session is later monitored. Lacey wouldn't dare try anything illegal. Now stay quiet and pay attention.'

Things were moving on the cot. The boy's voice had deepened, his face aged, he twisted as if to escape. Lacey's voice speared his armour.

'You have killed,' he said. 'You've admitted it. Now tell us about it. Tell us. Tell us.'

'Don't!' The scream wasn't that of a boy. 'Stop it! For God's sake stop it!'

'You will tell us?'

'Yes. Anything! I — ' The face twisted into sobs. Serge thrust himself forward.

'You are Frank Yendal?'

'Yes.'

'Tell us of the murder you committed.'

'Please!' The eyes were wild in the young-old face. 'It was during the war. I'd

250

killed before but this was different. We'd attacked and there was this Jerry. Only a kid. He had no gun, no nothing. He just stood there with his hands out. He was harmless. He wanted to surrender but I let him have the bayonet right through the guts. I don't know why I did it. I'd never done it before — not like that. Shooting, that was different, but never with a bayonet. Never an unarmed man. He screamed. It was horrible. I — I had to kick him to get the bayonet out.'

'And then?'

'Then I got caught in the wire.' The voice was dull now, lifeless. 'I hung there until the shells came. One of them blew off my legs. I can't remember dying.'

'When?'

'I don't know. Sometime during the war with Jerry.'

'The Jerry war?' Serge frowned. Brad stepped forward.

'1918,' he said softly. 'The First World War. Our troops called the Germans that.' He hesitated. 'May I ask him a question?'

'Go ahead.'

'Frank,' he said to the boy. 'Where did you fight?'

'France.'

'At what battle?'

'Lots of battles. Fighting all the time. The last at Wipers.'

Ypres! How had the boy known the soldiers' name for that little town in France? Brad felt Serge push him to one side as he spoke into the recorder.

'Completion of case. Investigation has shown that Frank Yendal, reborn James Allen Pertwen, committed the crime of murder before the statutory years of reincarnation and therefore cannot be punished and is of no concern to the temporal police.'

Brad could sympathize with his relief.

★　★　★

The tailor folded the final jacket, smoothed a suspected crease, deftly wrapped the garments into a compact bundle.

'There you are, sir,' he said cheerfully. 'Three suits of the best materials. One hundred and fifty imperials to pay.'

'You're positive they will fit?' Brad paused in his counting out the money. The tailer looked hurt.

'I would much rather have measured the gentleman myself,' he said. 'But all you gave me was a suit. Those I have made are perfect copies.' He hesitated. 'Better material, of course, but you did insist on that.'

'I know.' Brad pushed the heap of money into the waiting hand. 'Thanks for doing them so fast.'

'A moment, sir.' The tailor halted him as he reached the door. 'If you care for a suit for yourself, sir, I can guarantee the best fabric and workmanship in Phoenix.'

'I'll remember that.'

'And tell your friends,' yelled the tailor. He spoke to a closing door.

Outside Brad hefted the parcel. The clothes were for Serge, replacements of the suits he'd borrowed together with a bonus — it was time he started paying off some of his debts. He hesitated between walking or calling a cab. He decided on the cab. He'd been spending pretty freely lately but what the hell? Veldon was paying for it. And he had the feeling that he'd better not delay.

The feeling grew as he neared home. It was a mounting urgency as he paid off the driver. It was close to desperation as he reached the apartment. Throwing open the door he raced inside. And stopped.

Velda rose from a chair.

'Hello, there!'

'What do you want?'

'A little politeness would help. Where is our little Helen?'

'Working, I suppose. Why?'

'Nothing.' She smiled up into his face with a flash of white teeth. 'I just want to make sure that girl takes care of herself. And, in case you're wondering how I got in, I've got a key. Carl's key.'

'You didn't come here to tell me that,' he snapped. 'Suppose we get to the point. Did Veldon send you?'

'Such hurry!' She pursed her lips at him. 'Here we are, a man and a woman with time before us. Now who would ever believe that we did nothing but talk?'

'I don't know and I don't give a damn!'

Brad felt his fingernails driving into his palms. 'What do you want?'

'I've come to give you something.' Velda handed out an envelope. 'This. From Marc.'

He took the envelope and threw it on to a table. She followed it with her eyes.

'Aren't you going to open it?'

'Later.'

'As you like.' She hesitated. 'Marc said to tell you something. Three days.'

'So you've told me. Now beat it!'

'Are you throwing me out?' For a moment incredulity distorted the smooth lines of her face. Then, with a sudden change of emotion, she stepped close to him, resting her hands on his shoulders. The scent of her perfume was very strong.

'You're an odd man, Brad,' she said softly. 'Here I am, practically throwing myself at you, and all you can do is to show me the door. What's the matter, sweetheart? Don't you like me?'

'Do I have to?'

'What?'

'I don't remember Veldon making that

255

a part of our bargain,' said Brad flatly. Reaching up he jerked free her arms, and pushed her away. 'He said nothing about me having to make love to his messenger.'

She said something vile and swung her hand viciously at his face. He caught her wrist, stared coldly into her eyes.

'Get out of here, you damned vampire. You stink of death. And leave Helen alone. Do you understand me?' His knuckles whitened as he gripped her wrist. 'Leave her alone!'

He sighed as the door slammed behind her, wondering if he had made yet another mistake, not caring if he had. Weakly he leaned against the wall, fighting his inner torment. Strange how it was possible to live with pain, to become accustomed to it so that the grinding agony could be pushed into the background. Stranger still how a slight increase in that pain could be so overwhelming. But surely the relief given by the last dose should have lasted longer than it had?

He doubled with a grunting sigh of expelled breath and, crab-like, lurched into his bedroom. Glass shattered as he knocked over a tumbler. The bedside table went over with a crash. The mattress was a thing alive. He fought it, finally hurling it to one side to reveal the small, flat case hidden beneath.

Relief came with the prick of the hypodermic.

He sighed and put away the instrument and looked up, suddenly conscious of the disorder of the room.

And of Serge standing watching him from the open door.

★   ★   ★

'So there's no hope,' said the captain. 'Are you positive?'

'I've seen Maine about it a couple of times,' said Brad. 'He spoke of regrafts but it will take both time and money and I have neither.' He gave a humourless smile. 'Three hundred years waiting for a cure and I'm worse than when I started. We knew more about cancer in my time than they do now. In fact I was better off then. At least I didn't have to pay for my

257

treatment in advance.'

'Death was more important then,' said the captain.

'Death is still important — to me.'

'Yes, it would be.' Serge frowned down at the carpet. 'Does Helen know about this?'

'No, and she mustn't be told. That is something you must promise.'

'Why?'

'She has her own life to live and dead men have no part in it.'

'You aren't dead yet, Brad,' protested the captain. 'Helen could quite easily make a lot of money soon and I know that she'd want to help you.'

'How?' Brad squinted through a veil of smoke. 'I told you that there is no hope.'

'Perhaps not, but — ' Serge jerked to his feet and impatiently paced the floor. 'You were talking of the Cradle. Well, we have the same thing now. Stasis, you heard the lifeman talking about it. Now suppose — '

'I've thought about it,' said Brad tiredly. 'You don't think I sat down and folded my hands, do you? I enquired at the Institute. They are willing to co-operate but the terms are strictly cash in advance.'

'We could — I mean — ' Serge was foundering and Brad was in no mood for a recapitulation of the obvious.

'No!' He rose and looked out of the window. 'This talk is useless. Oh, I'm no hero and don't get the wrong impression but I'm a scientist and I've learned to accept facts. There is nothing either of you can do.'

'Helen — '

'Helen has debts and she's going to need her money to pay them off: She's got to pay them off. Serge, you've got to — '

He broke off as a key sounded in the lock. Helen entered the room. It was obvious to them both that she had been crying.

'I've lost my job,' she said. 'Sheeman was very polite about it but he said that he couldn't use either me or my designs. I — I've been wandering about ever since.'

'Can't use them?' Serge was incredulous. 'I don't understand this. You were a tremendous success.'

'That's what I thought.' Helen tried to smile, failed, gave up the attempt. 'Everyone seemed pleased. The buyers were full of interest. Then, when I called in today to discuss production and distribution, Sheeman broke the news.'

'Did he give any reason?' Brad was intent.

'No. He just said that circumstances beyond his control made it impossible to work with me.'

'Anything else?'

'Yes.' Helen paused, her eyes suspiciously bright. 'He hinted that it would be a waste of time for me to try getting work anywhere else. He said that none of the others would be interested in my designs.'

'I'll talk to him,' said Serge. 'There must be some mistake.'

'No mistake,' said Brad dryly. 'Sheeman knew what he was doing. Helen might as well follow his advice and save herself a lot of disappointment.'

It was Veldon, of course, the power behind the throne. He probably owned a controlling interest in Sheeman's business and had enough money and influence to

260

make the others dance to his tune. That was obvious but it dodged the question. Why should he want to keep Helen poor?

Brad lit a cigarette as he thought about it.

Pressure, of course, the same reason why he had shown Brad so much of his private intentions. The display of power and now the touch of iron force. He was determined that his chosen instrument would obey.

It seemed that he had little choice.

Numbly Brad sank into a chair, sensing the closing jaws of the trap, the relentless manipulation of a puppetmaster. Veldon was determined that he should get his own way. The irony of it should have been amusing. Brad Stevens, atomic physicist, once respected and admired and now, in this world, the thing for which he was most suited was to be a paid assassin.

But — why Helen?

Was it because Veldon imagined Brad would do anything to save her from his knives? Surely that cold manipulator of men would not place such a high value on sentiment? And, in any case, she was no longer his problem. Serge would take care of her so —

'Brad!' Helen leaned forward and touched his hand. 'Brad, are you feeling all right?'

'What?' He blinked and touched his forehead and found it beaded with sweat. He wondered what she had read in his face. 'Yes, I'm all right.'

'You looked distant,' she said. He managed to smile.

'I was just thinking.'

Was Velda after Helen's body?

Had she been promised it as a reward for faithful service? It made too much sense. Brad remembered how she had looked at Helen; her undisguised proprietary interest. And Veldon would take no risks. He would not submit to the operation until he was certain that it would succeed. On men as well as monkeys.

And what better test-subject could he have than a woman in a fresh, young body? A woman loyal because she was dependent and who would be willing to co-operate with his technicians to the last degree.

Velda's brain in Helen's body.

It could be the reason he wanted to grind her into debt.

'Brad!' It was Serge, his face anxious. 'Are you ill?'

'No.'

'Are you sure? You look ghastly. Is there anything I can do? Something I can get you?'

'No.' Brad was curt but he couldn't sit and exchange empty courtesies. Impatiently he rose and headed for his bedroom. Helen's voice halted him at the door.

'This envelope,' she said. 'Is it for me?'

'It's mine.' He snatched the forgotten envelope which Velda had given him and ripped it open. Inside were three objects. A card with a block-letter name and address. The torn halves of two one-thousand imperial banknotes.

It was enough.

The card to point the victim. The torn notes as promise of payment. And Velda had said that he had three days.

Three days to kill Eustace Emil Khan.

17

London had changed.

Picking his way through mounds of rubble, sweating in the confines of his anti-radiation suit, loaded with equipment, Brad wondered just what it was that made the city so different. Then, as Morgan stumbled and a metallic clang came from his gear, he knew. It was the silence.

London had never been silent. Not even the yearly two-minutes between the wars when everything had come to a stop had been like this. Then, at least, there had been the sounds of birds. Now there were no birds. This was the literal silence of the grave.

'Let's rest awhile.' Morgan slumped down on a kerb and glanced at the geiger counter strapped to his wrist. 'Are you sure you can trust these things?'

'I'm sure.' Brad sat beside him, checked his own, home-made instrument, opened the visor of his helmet. 'It's safe enough. Smoke?'

'Thanks.' The scavenger caught the cigarette, lit it, relaxed as he inhaled smoke. 'I never thought this would happen,' he said. 'When you gave me the thumbs down at the Folgone I thought that was the end of a good idea. You struck me as the type of man who, when he said no, meant it.'

'Things change,' said Brad. He drew on his cigarette. 'Why should anyone want to kill Khan?'

'Like who?'

'Marc Veldon.'

'That ghoul!' Morgan spat in the dust. 'He and Khan used to be partners way back. Something happened and they split up. Veldon reached for the sky but Khan didn't do so bad either.' He caught Brad's expression. 'Don't fall for his front. There's a lot more to him than that agency. If I had to make a guess I'd say that Veldon was sweetening him for something he knows. But maybe he could get tired of doling out the sugar.'

Tired — or scared that, with the

approach of senility, Khan could talk. Either way it fitted. Get Brad to kill Khan and so be rid of a danger. Drop a word in the right ear and have Brad in for quizzing. His association with Serge wouldn't do the captain any good and could provide the lever to part him from his position. Without work how could he help Helen?

It all came back to her.

But Brad hoped he could cut the spider's web which Veldon had spun.

'Not much danger here,' said Morgan cheerfully. He leaned back and stretched his thick legs. 'This area's been well covered. The cars went first.'

Brad had noticed the empty streets; looted for a metal-hungry civilization. The houses too had suffered. Even as he watched a portion of a roof fell in with a lifting cloud of dust. Salvage and weather had weakened the jerry-built fabric.

'That's something you've got to watch out for,' said Morgan casually. 'You've noticed that I walk in the centre of the road and that's one of the reasons. Any vibration can start a fall and it's no fun being buried under debris.'

Brad nodded, too conscious of the ache in his bones to enjoy banal conversation. He wished they could have gone by water but the dock area was impassable.

Morgan took a final drag at his cigarette and flipped away the butt.

'How much do you think we'll make?'

'You'll get a quarter of all we find,' said Brad curtly. 'That was our agreement.' He pulled a map from a pocket, opened it, pored over the sheet. 'We are here.' His finger rested on the map. 'We take this road and continue to here.'

'Almost due north?' Morgan looked puzzled. 'There's nothing in that area unless you've specialized knowledge.'

'I have, but I'm not interested in the north. We are going right into the centre.' Brad heard the sharp intake of Morgan's breath. 'Scared, Morgan?'

'Sure I'm scared. It's hot in there.'

'I know, but that's where the money is. To get it we've got to take a chance. Now, if we reach the tube at Gants Hill we can follow the lines into the City.' Slowly he folded the map. 'We can't go overland,' he explained. 'These suits aren't all that good and we'd collect a lethal dose before we got there. Underground we stand a chance. It's the only one we've got.'

He tucked the map back into his pocket, rose, adjusted the visor of his helmet. Morgan hadn't moved.

'Are you coming?' Brad shifted his equipment to a less uncomfortable position. 'Or are you going to sit there feeling sorry for yourself?'

'You tricked me,' said Morgan slowly. 'You didn't say anything about going into the centre.'

'I didn't trick you. I told you there was a fortune to be made and I knew how to make it. There is and I do.' Brad tightened a strap. 'Now let's go and get it.'

★ ★ ★

It was a long walk to Gants Hill. Twice they halted for rest, once for food, and as it began to grow dark they reached their destination.

Morgan hesitated at the entrance to the Underground.

268

'How far?'

'About ten miles.' Brad thrust past him into the station. 'Come on. I've been over this route a hundred times.'

But that had been before the Débâcle when bright lights had edged the platforms and cheerful posters had relieved the monotony of the walls. Now there was nothing but darkness and decay; the air heavy with stagnation and foetid odours. And things looked different in the beam of his flashlight.

He started as the light shone on a looming bulk, then grunted as he recognized a ticket machine. Something darted across the edge of the beam, sinister in the shadow.

'Spider.' Morgan's voice boomed in the stillness. 'Nasty brutes.'

A spider?

So big?

Brad wondered what other freaks of mutation would be waiting for them in the lower regions.

Cautiously he led the way down the motionless escalator. The platform, deep buried, had escaped most of the ravages of climatic change, but something had robbed the walls of posters and maps. Quickly Brad oriented himself, dropped down to the tracks, stood looking up at Morgan.

'Come on,' he ordered. 'This is the way.' He gestured with his flashlight. Rust-red rails glowed in the light of the beam. 'We follow these straight into the City.'

The scavenger hesitated. Brad wondered if the man suffered from claustrophobia. The truth was more bizarre.

'I don't like this.' Morgan jumped down and began to walk at Brad's side. 'I was trapped underground once. In a mine. We only had a couple of candles.'

'A coal mine?'

'Tin. In Cornwall. The roof had caved in and cut us off. We could hear the rescue party trying to reach us. They didn't try for long. Not that I can blame them, the shaft was dangerous and they didn't even know for sure that we hadn't been caught in the fall. So we just sat there waiting for them to try again.'

'Did they?'

'I don't know. The candles gave out and that's all I remember. I suppose they just left us there.' Morgan tripped and almost fell. 'Blast! I could have broken a leg.'

'Stay behind me,' ordered Brad. 'Tread in the centre of the sleepers; the ends are mostly rotten.'

He heard the scavenger fall in behind him and pushed on through the tunnel. The going was uneven, the walls scabrous, mottled with damp and fretted with sagging plaster. Snake-like wires trailed along the walls and the air held a thick, dead quality which made it hard to breathe.

His light gleamed on something ahead.

It was a train, the wheels rusted to the rails, the doors and windows still intact. Curiously Brad squinted through the windows as he squeezed past, half-expecting to find the compartments filled with a skeletal load of commuters. He saw nothing. Just the bare metal and dirty plastic. Even the straps had gone from the roof.

'Rats.' Morgan gestured to where ruby glints winked at the edge of illumination.

'God help us if we get hurt.'

Brad echoed his prayer as he stared at the thing caught in the beam of his flashlight.

The rats had changed. The thing before him was big, sleek and bold. The eyes which shone beneath the enlarged skull were alive with intelligence. It sat, not as a rodent, but as an ape.

It chittered as Brad moved, vanishing with a flash of brown fur, the whip of a naked, prehensile tail. For the first time Brad understood why he had seen no bones.

There had been ten million people in London at the time of the Débâcle. There could have been few survivors. A handful scattered at the extreme perimeter of the city. The rest had died. Some from the volatalizing effects of the atom bombs. A few by fire, accident and panic. The rest from the invisible storm of neutrons which had left the buildings intact while destroying all life.

Ten million people. Mummified, perhaps withered, all sterile from corruptive bacteria.

No wonder the rats had survived.

Brad stumbled and fell against Morgan, who had taken the lead. The scavenger had halted, the beam of his light directed at the curving roof, the blotched encrustations. Black earth showed in a rising mound beneath which were buried the rust-red rails.

'Fall-in.' Morgan's voice sounded flatly from his helmet. 'The tunnel's blocked. We'll have to go back.'

Brad frowned, trying to remember the lay-out of the system. They had walked for hours, passing Mile End, which was their closest junction. They were following the Central Line. The Metropolitan ran above ground, which ruled it out. The District would take them through the complex of Whitechapel, which was highly radioactive. This was their only route.

He said so and Morgan swore.

'For God's sake, Brad! The tunnel's blocked. Can't you see that?'

'I can see it — and I can see something else.' Brad picked up a stone, threw it at a pair of ruby eyes. The rat squeaked and scuttled over the mound of debris. 'The rats get through.'

'We aren't rats.'

'No, but maybe there's a little space at the top. Certainly there must be a hole. It's possible that we could crawl through it.'

He stepped past Morgan and began to climb the obstruction. The dirt was loosely packed. A little of it fell from hands and feet as he pulled himself upwards. His helmet touched the roof. He slithered sideways and found a hole. It was small but it would have to do.

'All right,' he called down to Morgan. 'I'll go ahead. You stay close behind.'

Dog-like he began to dig his way through the mound. He clawed the dirt from in front, sweeping it to the rear, shoving head and shoulders into the narrow gap. He flexed his body like a worm as he moved forward. He tried not to think of the tons of soil above or how far the obstruction could extend.

'Brad!' Morgan was in trouble. 'Brad! I'm stuck!'

They were in a narrow cleft between the roof and the top of the mound. It was impossible for Brad to turn.

'Try wriggling,' he ordered. 'Or back out and shift your pack.'

The dirt trembled to the vibration of frantic movement.

'It's no good!' Morgan sounded on the edge of hysteria. 'The dirt's collapsed behind me. I can't free my legs. Help me, Brad!'

'Not so loud!'

Brad held his breath as he sensed the movement of dirt above his head. A soft ripping sound came from one side. A lump of rotten concrete fell somewhere with a soggy thud. Behind him Morgan whimpered as the dirt closed tighter around his legs.

Brad tore at the soil, found his flashlight, held it before him. The beam shone on a rusted piece of metal sticking from the roof. Beyond it the passage widened into the open tunnel. Scant feet separated them from safety.

'Get your arms before you,' he said quietly to Morgan. 'Grip my ankles. Right?'

He felt the death-grip of the scavenger's big hands.

'Now listen. I'm going to hang on to a beam. When I give the word pull yourself clear. Once through and we're safe. Ready now?'

He reached forward and locked his hands around the scrap of rusted metal.

'Pull!'

The pain was excruciating. Brad felt as if he were being stretched on a medieval rack.

'Again!'

Gritting his teeth Brad heaved on the metal as Morgan pulled at his legs. He heard a slither, a grunt of relief and then the rattle of dirt on his helmet.

'The roof! Hurry!'

Once more came the savage pull then, suddenly, Morgan was free. Frantically Brad clawed his way past the scrap of metal, felt something yield beneath his weight, felt something else slam into him from above. Together he and Morgan rolled down a slope followed by an avalanche of dirt and stone.

'Quick.' Morgan jerked to his feet and

pulled Brad clear of the rubble. 'Move before the rest comes down.'

'The flashlight.' Brad snatched up a stone, swore, threw it away. 'I've lost my flashlight.'

'To hell with it.' Morgan jerked him along the tunnel. 'Hurry!'

They made it just in time. Tripping, stumbling in the darkness they somehow managed to keep ahead of the flood of debris pouring from the shattered roof.

'Well,' said Morgan as the echoes died away. 'That's one route we won't be taking back home. Are you hurt?'

'No.' Brad cursed as he tripped and fell. 'Where's your flashlight?'

'Back with yours. I didn't stop to pick it up.' A tiny beam cut the darkness. 'This is my emergency light. Stop a minute while I check your suit.'

Brad waited as the scavenger looked him over.

'Nothing torn,' he said and handed Brad the light. 'Check me out.' He waited until Brad gave the all clear. 'Well, that's something to be grateful for. If those rats ever caught the scent of food we wouldn't stand a snowball's chance in hell. How are you physically?'

'Rough.'

'We can't do anything about that now. How much farther have we to go?'

'About a mile and a half. Maybe two miles.'

'Then let's get on with it.' Morgan headed down the tunnel. 'This flashlight isn't all that strong and I'd hate to be caught down here in the dark.'

The ruby glints crept closer as he spoke.

They emerged at Chancery Lane. It was dawn when they reached the street, the pale light in the east softening the effects of time and destruction so that, to Brad, everything seemed painfully familiar. Then he saw the ranked cars; heaps of rust beside their guardian meters, the wreckage in the road, the trees thrusting at shattered concrete, the thousand eyes of empty windows.

He raised his arm and looked at the counter on his wrist. The wind was from the west and it was hot. It had always been hot. The heat of too many people squeezed into too small a space. The tropic warmth of a furious desire for wealth and a place in the sun.

But this time it was a different kind of heat.

18

'Hot,' said Morgan. He scowled at his geiger. 'Well, we expected that. How long have we got?'

'Not long.' Brad hesitated. 'Look, I know how to read these things. A guildsman wouldn't let you stay in this area a minute longer than you had to. And he'd be right. That damn wind's loaded.'

'So what? I'm willing to take a chance if you are. Let's stop wasting time.' Morgan took a step forward, halted, baffled at not knowing where to go. 'Where do we find the loot?'

'Around the corner.' Brad led the way to Hatton Garden. Morgan wasn't impressed.

'Here?'

'That's right.' Brad gestured down the unpretentious street, the insignificant buildings. 'This area used to be the heart of the diamond industry. If there are any stones in London this is where you'll find them.'

'Where do we start?' grunted Morgan. He was still unconvinced.

'The Bourse would be best but any of the buildings should yield what we're after. Can you open a safe?'

Morgan grinned and patted his equipment.

'All right,' said Brad. 'Let's get to work. Uncut diamonds look like ordinary stones so don't make the mistake of leaving them behind.'

'I know a diamond when I see one.' Brad had touched the scavenger's professional pride. 'What will you be doing?'

'I'll work with you. While you tackle the safes I'll be clearing the benches.' Brad looked again at his counter. Here they were sheltered a little from the wind but the level was still far too high. 'We'll have to hurry.'

'I'm waiting.'

Morgan was impatient. Brad looked at the parked cars, the unshuttered windows. The bombs must have arrived during the day, probably in the late afternoon. He pointed to a building which still bore traces of flaking gold lettering.

'We'll start with that one.'

'Right.' Morgan reached out, gripped Brad as he stepped forward. 'Me first,' he said. 'I know what I'm doing, you don't. These old buildings can be death-traps. I'll go ahead and test the structure.'

The building was sound. Brad slowly climbed the stairs and passed through an open door. It was a heavy, fireproof door lined with painted steel. Within double-glazed windows glowed the light of early dawn. The glass had shattered into a million shards but the wire-mesh of the armoured glass had held them in place. The air was dry and stale. At long benches running down the centre of the room yellowed figures sat or slumped in a parody of sleep.

'Bones,' whispered Morgan. He pushed one of the bodies to one side. It had been a woman, young from the plastic beads around the neck, the gay colours of the dress. Now it was old and sere, shrivelled like a mummy from an Egyptian tomb.

'The rats couldn't get in,' whispered Morgan. 'I had to force the door.' He looked at the ranked corpses. 'What were they doing here?'

He was whispering, not from respect but for fear of undue vibration. Unnecessary here, perhaps, but a part of his ingrained training. Brad followed his example.

'They were probably sorting, cutting or polishing gems.' He leaned over a withered figure and took something from his hand. 'This one was polishing.' He straightened and looked towards the end of the room. An office faced him with glassless windows. 'The safe must be in there. Get to it while I clear these benches.'

★   ★   ★

It became a treasure hunter's dream come true.

It was a simple matter of looking and picking and not having to choose what to take. And, if the dead watched, it was easy to ignore them. Brad collected from the benches while, as he worked, the fierce hiss of controlled fire came from the safe as Morgan forced open the boxes with chemical heat.

It grew into a pattern. Like two vultures they ranged the famous street and took what they found.

'A fortune!' Morgan shook the diamond-heavy bag at his waist. 'Brad, I've got to hand it to you. You certainly knew where the loot was to be found.'

'I told you that.'

'I know.' Morgan hefted the bag again, his beard split by a grin. 'But when you've heard as much guff as I have you get cynical. I've listened to a dozen propositions from men who swore they had the secret of compact loot and who would give me the directions for a cut in the profit. But this — !'

He blew out his cheeks and Brad felt a quick sympathy.

'A nice feeling, isn't it?'

'Nice!' Morgan shook his head. 'Man, you simply don't know. I've risked life and limb for more years than I like to remember and I've been lucky to stay ahead. Damn it, Brad, every scavenger born dreams of something like this. Some make it. Tog Halsen for one. He found your vault and retired to a farm in

Ireland. Now it's my turn.'

'Yes,' said Brad dryly. 'But it's not going to do you any good unless you get back alive.' He looked at the indicator on his suit. They had already stayed too long. He said so. Morgan shrugged.

'We can buy treatment,' he said. 'Anyhow, which way do we go?'

'North.' Brad frowned over his map. 'We can work our way underground on the Victoria Line and follow the tracks well beyond the City. Then we swing east and south. It will be a long trip and the sooner we get started the better.'

'And leave all this?' Morgan's gesture embraced the unlooted safes.

'You've run out of thermite,' reminded Brad. 'If you use explosives you could bring down the building.'

'Maybe.' Morgan was thoughtful as he examined one of the buildings. 'That place seemed pretty sound to me when I investigated. No stones on the benches so they must all be in the safe. It's a big safe, Brad. I'm going to crack it.'

He was gone before Brad could protest.

He sighed, leaning against a sagging lamp-post, knowing that the scavenger would never leave until he had made his attempt. He checked his indicator and shrugged. A little longer wouldn't do any harm. How much poison is too much?

'I've set it.' Morgan panted with effort as he ran from the building and rejoined Brad. 'A long fuse and a small charge but I've placed it just right and it should work fine. It should blast in — ' he looked at his watch ' — twelve seconds.' He began to count. 'Five — four — three — two — one — now!'

Nothing happened.

'Damn! It must have gone out.'

'Wait!' Brad grabbed at the scavenger as he headed towards the building. He knew of the vagaries of explosive and how the most carefully made fuse could be unreliable at times. 'Give it longer,' he urged. 'Double at least.'

They gave it double. Treble. Then Morgan lost patience and shook himself free of Brad's restraining grip.

'It's gone out,' he decided. 'I'll fit a new fuse.'

The charge exploded five seconds after he entered the building.

★   ★   ★

It wasn't loud but it didn't have to be; the noise came from the collapsing structure, a long, sickening rumble followed by a tearing crash which threw dust high into the air and cast a gritty fog over the sun.

'Morgan!'

Shaken, bruised by the sudden rain of brick, tiles and weathered cornice, Brad wiped clean his visor and ran towards the wreckage. Squinting through the dust he peered into a mess of splintered beams, plaster and rubble beneath which Morgan would be lying. He could be dead, probably was, but Brad had to make sure.

'Morgan!'

Doggedly he began to tear at the mound of shattered brick.

Morgan was alive. He lay, a thick beam across his back, his legs buried in rubble and one arm twisted at an impossible angle. He was trapped and he knew it.

'Brad!' His voice held a liquid quality and a froth of blood stained his beard. 'Don't touch anything,' he warned. 'The whole lot could come down at any second.'

'I've got to get you out of here.' Brad looked around, found a splintered length of wood, shoved it beneath the beam and heaved upwards. A rain of broken plaster fell from above. He heaved again, red flecks staining his vision. The beam shifted a little, rose, bore down with crushing weight. 'Hurry! Drag yourself free!'

He heard a scratching, dragging sound then the wood he was using as a lever snapped. Released from the upward pressure the beam thudded back into its bed. Falling rubble reached to Brad's feet.

'Morgan!'

The scavenger had done his best. He had managed to drag himself a little forward before the falling beam had smashed his legs. He was still trapped.

'I'll try again,' promised Brad. 'I'll get

something stronger.'

'No.' Morgan reached out and gripped his arm. 'It wouldn't do any good. I'm numb from the waist down. I guess my back is broken and it's certain my ribs are.' He coughed a crimson stream. 'Lungs punctured.'

'Relax. I'll soon have you out.'

'No.' The scavenger shook his head. 'It's no good, Brad, this is the end of the line for me.' He began to laugh, coughed instead, then managed a grin. 'Damn the luck,' he wheezed. 'Twice on the trot I've been buried alive. But this time I can see the sun. I'm learning. Maybe, one day, I'll have more sense.'

He fumbled at his waist with his good arm, thrust the diamond-heavy bag towards Brad.

'Listen,' he wheezed. 'You take the loot. I've a wife and kids back in Phoenix. Khan will know how to find them. See they get my share.'

'They'll get it,' promised Brad.

'Thanks.' The scavenger coughed and fought for breath. 'My chest! I'm burning — ' He coughed again and the visor of his helmet darkened with a ruby flood.

Brad opened it, wiped the bearded mouth and the sweat-dewed forehead. He looked at the trapping beam, the heap of rubble delicately balanced above. He had been lucky. If he tried to release Morgan again he would bury them both.

'You'll have to make it alone,' gasped the scavenger. 'Go overland. You'll never make it through the tunnels without a light. Watch out for rotten manholes. Keep clear of buildings. Stay well away from the sewers. Keep an eye on your geiger . . . you'll have to find water . . . keep on your . . . be careful . . . Khan . . .'

Brad wiped the contorted face.

'Khan! Give him my share. He's straight.'

'I'll see to it, Morgan. If I get through.'

'You'll get through.' Blood welled from his mouth as Morgan tried to grin. 'Diamonds,' he gasped. 'More money than I thought existed. Funny, isn't it? I'll laugh about it later.' He choked back a groan.

Brad inched back, unzipped his suit,

drew out a small, flat case. Carefully he lifted the hypodermic and stared at the remaining morphine. Morgan was dying and in agony. The morphine couldn't save him but it could ease his passage. Deftly he administered the injection.

'What?' Morgan stirred at the prick of the needle. 'What are you doing?'

'Something to take away the pain,' said Brad. He replaced the hypodermic and tried not to think of his own need. 'Something to make you sleep.'

'Sleep? I'm dying!'

'Yes.'

'Dying,' murmured the scavenger. 'Well, it couldn't last forever and it was time for a change. At least I died rich.' He managed to grin as the drug took effect. 'Better luck the next time, eh?'

'Sure.'

'There's always a next time,' said Morgan drowsily. He lifted his head with sudden terror. 'Brad! The rats! If you leave before — the rats!'

'I won't leave,' soothed Brad. 'And they won't get you.'

'But — '

'That's a promise, Morgan. I keep my promises.'

'Yes,' said the scavenger. He was almost asleep. 'I guess that you do.' He drew a long, shuddering breath. 'So long,' he muttered. 'I'll be seeing you — sometime.'

It was dark when Brad began the long journey home. A pale moon hung in the sky and, behind him, sending a thin plume of smoke into the sky, the flame of the funeral pyre sent shadows dancing in the street.

19

Without lights and alone it was impossible to go underground. The river was out. Brad had to weave his way overland between the areas of greatest devastation.

By the pale light of the moon he studied his map. It was a Guild map belonging to Morgan and it showed splotches of red, yellow and blue. Too many splotches and too vague in outline. He was surrounded by areas of potential death.

He checked his indicator and wondered why he was worried.

He was already dying, of cancer if not from radiation, and it was now only a question of time. But he had to get back to Phoenix with the looted diamonds. They would save Helen if not himself. It was the only way he could beat Veldon.

He headed south, crossing the river at Blackfriars, pausing to look down into the crystal water. Something moved in the limpid stream and he hurried on. The radioactive hell of the dock area wasn't the only hazard to river-travel.

Walworth Road stretched wide and straight from the end of the bridge. At the Elephant and Castle his geiger warned him of what lay ahead. He turned west and ran into the devastation around Westminster. He turned east and veered to the south again. If he could dodge the worst areas and reach the suburbs he could swing east and head in a wide circle towards the north. It would be a long, hard trip but, given time, he could make it.

Securing the precious bag to his belt he set out along the deserted roads. They were pale and shadowed in the moon-light, deceptive stretches which looked all the same, an endless maze of brick and concrete and marching buildings.

First he got lost.

Then he wandered into nightmare.

There was a time of madness when he had entered every drug store in a vain effort to find pain-easing morphine. He had gone wild with frustration, fumbling in the darkness sending phials, ampoules crashing to the ground. Somewhere in the litter could be the drug he sought. But the labels had rotted away or become so discoloured as to be unreadable.

He had experienced thirst so intense that he had run like a dog, lapping at puddles, staggering from one to the other through a succession of hallucinations; fountains, water-troughs, fish-ponds, running gutters and smooth slabs of ice.

There had been the endless sensation of being watched and the final, terrible disorientation so that he seemed to wander, an outcast in time, the warped trees springing from the concrete mingling and blending with the streets and houses. It was as if the distant past had somehow merged with his remembered present.

And there had been a fire.

It burned all alone in a small hollow in a sheltered place among the debris of a house. A small, carefully built fire with a wide frill of dead ash and a thin column of smoke rising from the smouldering fuel. A heap of splintered wood lay to one side, shards of bone stacked close to the kindling, and both wood and bone showed the marks of rodent teeth.

That had been during the day — which one he wasn't sure but that night there had been pale shapes staring at him from the tops of trees and from upper windows. Odd, terrifying shapes like bleached apes who watched and tittered and vanished when he shouted.

And, the following day, there had been the thing in the sky. The grotesque swollen thing which hummed and swooped down and wouldn't go away.

And from which there had been no escape.

'A Guild mapping patrol found you.' Serge sat at the side of the bed, his profile clear against the soft green of the curtained window. 'They were checking the southern region of the city in an airship and saw something move. They dropped to investigate. It was you.'

'Where?' Brad was mildly curious.

'Far south. Near Eltham.'

'When?'

'Twenty-three hours ago. From what we can gather you were wandering about

296

the city for over forty hours. You were delirious when they found you. They gave you dope and emergency therapy then brought you here to the Institute.'

'The diamonds?'

'Safe.'

Brad sighed and relaxed against his pillow. He was conscious of a peculiar numbness of his body as if the nerves had been paralysed. He felt no pain — not even the texture of the sheets. Beside the bed a squat, humming machine was attached to his body by pipes buried in the wall of his chest. He touched them. They were rigid with internal pressure. He looked at Serge.

'A blood-wash,' explained the captain. 'You've had a tremendous dose of radiation. They've been passing fresh blood through your body ever since you arrived.'

Brad nodded, idly wondering how much the service cost, then dismissed the thought. Money meant nothing now that he had returned with the gems.

'Helen?'

'She's waiting outside.' Serge leaned

closer, his face serious. 'Brad, I've got to know. What happened to Morgan?'

'Dead.' Brad shook his head at the captain's look of anxiety. 'No, I didn't kill him. He was trapped and died in a falling building.' He remembered his promise to the scavenger. 'A quarter of what I carried goes to his wife and kids. Khan will handle it.'

'I'll attend to it.'

'The rest goes to Helen. Buy her debts back from Veldon and see to it that she never wants for anything. That neither of you want for anything.' Brad managed a smile. 'Call it a wedding present.'

'It's a tremendous fortune.'

He didn't argue about it or give his thanks. Then Brad saw the tight lines around the captain's mouth and knew the reason. Serge wasn't being impolite — there simply wasn't time.

'I'm dying?'

'Yes, Brad.'

'I see.' Brad picked idly at the covers. He felt a curious detachment as if he stood to one side and watched himself. So he was was going to die? So what? All men had to die. Serge cleared his throat.

'There isn't a chance, Brad. I'm not going to lie and pretend there is. You've got cancer and that's bad enough, but you won't die from it. Radiation poisoning will kill you within hours.'

Brad wondered why he sounded so depressed. Death should have meant nothing to a man of this age. Then he remembered that Serge was a cripple. He couldn't be certain that death was not the final ending. He knew but was not certain, personally certain. He lacked the experience which would be proof.

Like Brad himself.

Leaning back he thought about it. He had been so convinced that reincarnation was a myth. Yet he was a scientist who had to face facts. Could he have been wrong?

There had been a boy who spoke like a man and who had known something no boy of this age could have known. Wipers, he'd said. The soldiers' name for Ypres. How had he known?

And Veldon believed.

Grenmae had no doubts.

Morgan had been positive.

All the men and women who conducted their lives on the basis of the warm conviction that they had lived and would live again — could they all be wrong?

Brad sighed. He wished now that he'd not been so quick to doubt. At least he could have tried the reversal techniques for himself. But he had never had the money and, when he did, things had happened too fast. And there had been another reason. Suppose they had not worked? Would he have been content to assume he was a cripple?

Brad suddenly thought of Carl.

He had been convinced.

How much proof did a man need before he was willing to accept the obvious?

*   *   *

The door opened and Helen entered the room. She had been crying, her eyes were red with tears, but now they were dry and shining with hope. Maine walked beside her and he was smiling.

'Brad,' said Helen. 'Listen to me. There isn't much time so you mustn't interrupt or argue. You returned with the largest fortune ever known in this age. And, in this world, money can buy anything.'

'It's for you and Serge.'

'We'll take all we need.' Helen, like Serge, didn't waste time with thanks. 'The rest is for you.'

'For a dead man?' Brad shook his head. 'Are you crazy, Helen? What would I do with it?'

'Use it,' she snapped. 'You're not dead yet and you've nothing to lose. I can't just stand and watch you die. It was bad enough when there was no hope but now — ' She broke off and looked at Maine. 'Please tell him.'

'Certainly.' The lifeman smiled down at Brad. 'It's really quite simple,' he said. 'We have a stasis service which is now in functional order. It will be a simple matter to seal you in a capsule for a few years until the effects of your over-exposure have dissipated. Continual blood-wash, slowing of the metabolism, the introduction of counter-radioactives — we have a good technique. Expensive, but good.'

'I don't doubt it,' said Brad dryly. 'So you cure me of radiation poisoning. Then what?'

'The cancer is a different matter. I propose to tackle it in two ways. First we will inaugurate a crash-programme into the cause and cure of your affliction. Second there is a theory of my own which I think offers a high probability of success. And, of course, there are always the regrafting techniques.'

'A brain transplant?'

Maine blinked his surprise.

'Maybe you've never thought about it,' said Brad. 'You should. If not you'll be left behind in the race. Veldon can tell you about it.' He looked at Serge. 'You said that I was going to die.'

The captain didn't answer.

'He thought that you were,' said Helen. 'We both thought so. Even the lifeman who attended you offered no hope. Then I remembered who resurrected us. With your money you have hope.'

Money! It all came back to that.

It was odd now that he simply didn't care. He tried to smile and saw her eyes widen. He didn't know that his attempt had looked like the rictus of death.

'Brad!'

'Allow me.' Maine stepped forward and checked the humming machine. He rested the tips of his fingers on Brad's throat and checked the readings of a small instrument he applied to various parts of his body. Helen touched his arm.

'Well?'

'We have little time.'

'I see.' With an effort she mastered her emotion. 'Please commence your preparations without delay. Brad, you must give me your attested deposition to use your money in any way that I see fit. It would also be best to give me full ownership of your body.'

Give her his body.

He tried to smile and saw by her expression that he hadn't made it. He tried to tell her that but found it impossible to speak. It was as if the boney hand of Death, impatient for his elusive victim, was slowly and relentlessly closing about his throat.

'Maine!'

The lifeman took her place and did something with a needle. It didn't hurt but the hand eased from his windpipe and air rushed into his lungs.

Then there was the recorder and a notary and a droning preamble. He heard his own voice, strange and oddly liquid, gasping words into a grilled mouth which gaped from the end of a flexible neck.

* * *

There was peace.

There was a bustle of activity all around him but he rested tranquil in the centre of the storm. And the tranquillity was helped by the fact that all this was familiar. He had gone through all this before.

'It won't be long now.' Maine smiled down at his prize subject. 'You know, Stevens, you are a very fortunate man.'

Brad blinked his eyes, too sleepy to speak, too comfortable to do anything but lie and stare at the ceiling.

'We'll take good care of you,' continued Maine. 'The best that money can provide. You don't have a thing to worry about and I honestly mean that. When you wake your troubles will be over.'

Then he was gone and two others occluded the light.

'Brad!' Helen was crying. 'Oh, Brad!'

'He can't speak,' said Serge. He put out his hand and rested it against Brad's shoulder. 'This isn't the end,' he said. 'Sometime, in the future, we'll all meet again.'

It was, thought Brad, the most comforting philosophy ever discovered in any age. Death was not an end, but a transition. Not to an invented Heaven or Hell but to a familiar world with familiar things and the possibility of meeting old friends.

Helen, perhaps?

She stooped and kissed him full on the lips.

'Goodbye, Brad. I'll never forget you.'

Then she was gone and Maine was back, still smiling but with a trace of worry behind the smile as if he were a man racing against time and not daring to let the clock know that he was its competitor.

'Time to go now,' he said. 'Give my regards to the future and, remember, you have nothing to worry about.'

Nothing.

Nothing at all.

Nothing but death and that was a dream.

He would live again.

THE END

Along with a large cash legacy, Miss Alice Ames had inherited the Whistling Sands, an old house overlooking the Conway Estuary. And it was here she began married life with Wally Somers — alias Wally Sloane, wanted by the Sydney police. To Wally, Alice and the Whistling Sands were just a means to the money he stood to gain. But when both had come to mean more to him than that, he became enmeshed in a web of deceit — and murder . . .

PLACE MILL

Barbara Softly

In 1645, the Civil War rages and young Nicholas Lambert joins the Royalist Army, leaving his sister Katharine behind. Six years later, with the Royalists defeated, Nicholas is a fugitive. Returning home for safety, accompanied by two friends, he finds much has changed. Taking Katharine and his cousin Hester as cover, they attempt to escape to France, but encounter difficulties before even reaching the coast. And then Katharine disappears . . . Suspicious of their new acquaintances, who will they be able to trust?

DEAD WEIGHT

E. C. Tubb

Sam Falkirk, Captain in the World Police stationed at the World Council in New York, investigates the death of Angelo Augustine, a Council employee. Superficially a parcel courier, Angelo had also spied for Senator Rayburn, whose power-hungry plan is the destruction of the Orient. Meanwhile, Senator Sucamari of the Japanese legation has a deadly plan himself, involving a parcel containing a Buddha coated with enough bacteria to cause a plague across the Americas. When the parcel is stolen can Falkirk find the criminal in time?

ONE FOR THE ROAD

Peter Conway

After a car accident shatters the lives of Mike and Penny Craven, the ex-racing car driver's morale is low. However, when he sees a young woman attacked by thugs and rescues her, his life begins to take on a new meaning. But soon his courage, his skill as a driver and his marriage are all called into question as he and the young woman face violence and death at the hands of a group of vicious criminals.

TO LOVE AND PERISH

Ernest Dudley

In Castlebay, North Wales, Dick Merrill is on trial, accused of murdering his wife. Merrill, good looking and attractive, is fatally in love with Margot Stone, who is herself already married. Philip Vane, a lawyer whose career was mysteriously ruined, finds himself similarly infatuated with Margot when he becomes personally involved in Merrill's sensational murder-trial. A shadowy figure, Vane's participation in the trial is twisted and erratic — will the outcome be as unpredictable?